A Deadly Fae Duology Novella

Your paragraph text

SPRING

Book 1.5

CASSANDRA ASTON

CONTENTS

CONTENT & TRIGGER WARNINGS

This book is a work of fiction. No part of this book should be construed as true or accurate; no people or animals were harmed in the creation of this story. Spring is intended for mature readers and is recommended for 18+. Mature content and triggers are listed below.

Descriptions of torture and death

Allusions to rape and other acts of sexual deviance

Open door spice

Biting and blood

References to fae, fairies and other fantastical creatures

Explicit language

Mental and physical issues described

Please use caution when reading.

To the readers who wanted more of Kaspar's story.
Just remember you asked for this.

PRESENT DAY

Kaspar

A little known fact when reading the deadly fae duology. There are three versions of Mira's death. What you may have read in Whispers Among Thorns if you read an early copy, what's written in the history books—and the truth...

*B*lood bloomed in the water, a deep indigo cloud drifting from my sister Mira's wound. Sightless eyes stared at nothing as it spread, blocking the light. I reached for her–

I woke with a gasp, eyes flying wide as I took in my surroundings.

– A passage from Whispers Among Thorns

CHAPTER 1

Kaspar

More than two and a half centuries ago.

"Sav! Wait!"

I crashed through the thick underbrush, swiping low-hanging branches aside with a wave of my hand. Auburn hair streamed behind her as she ran at breakneck speed. I chased her, but on land, I was no match for her. She'd had years of racing through forests and marshes after all, and I had need of legs only when visiting her.

Trees in shades of green and orange bloomed to life as she passed. Bows dipped low to lend her strength as she dodged and wove with a grace only held by those of the fae courts. She wasn't royalty, but it must have been an oversight when they were drawing family names. Sav was every bit a princess.

The pads of my feet, strange in this body, sunk into spongy moss, and I ducked instinctively when a pair of leather wings launched from a gnarled branch. Soft morning light trickled through the canopy, warming my cool skin, my lips stretched into a wide grin.

Out here, far from court and the prying eyes of my uncle, I didn't have to measure every breath. My steps could falter. My laugh could slip, if only for a moment. My kind, water fae, had cold skin and colder hearts. We didn't have the same emotions warm-blooded land creatures clung to. When something delighted us, it was a superficial thing, a fleeting moment of satisfaction quickly chased away by unfeeling indifference.

At least that's how my mother described it.

I still remembered the first time she scolded me for my temper. I was five, maybe four, and had screamed my outrage when she and father planned a trip to the surface to meet with the royals of the spring court. She'd pinched the point of my ear and dragged me into a room off the main hall.

"You must regulate yourself, Kaspar. A sea fae does not conduct himself in such a manner."

My lower lip jutted out, and I crossed my arms over my chest. "Because I'm a prince?"

One of my mother's slender eyebrows lifted as her gaze trailed my glimmering turquoise scales. "Because you're water folk."

I hadn't understood what she meant then. But over the next several years, I learned to swallow feelings whole. Court voices never rose, never trembled. I trained mine to match. But it wasn't until I was eleven that I truly accepted how different I was—when my parents died and I wasn't expected to feel anything about it.

A crash sounded ahead, and in moments, I stumbled over a heaving mass of auburn strands. I rolled off her, swallowing my grin as I took her in—shaking with laughter; hair full of leaves.

"You're positively wild," I said, covering my glee with the mild amusement expected of my kind.

Sav lifted onto her elbows, exhaling a whoosh of air. It did little to uncover her face from the mane she was drowning in. Sitting up, I parted her hair, exposing soft pink lips stretched into a smile and red cheeks.

"You move like a snail." She laughed.

I leaned back to give her space, and she sat up, twisting her tangled locks into a braid and tossing it over her shoulder.

"Let's race in the lake next time and see who wins."

4

She shoved my arm, sending warmth trickling through my bare skin. "I can't breathe underwater. Remember?"

"I could breathe for us both." My heart sped, but I kept my face impassive.

Her cheeks flamed, and she jumped to her feet, dusting off her skirts and turning away from me. "Come on. I want to see how close we can get."

I stood. "Sav... I can't."

She whipped around, eyeing me. "Scared?"

I shook my head, waving a hand over velvet slacks to remove the moss and leaves clinging to the fabric. "No. I represent my court. I wouldn't be a fae trespassing in another prince's court. I would be a prince declaring either war or an alliance with another principality."

Sav frowned, twisting her finger through a loose strand of hair. "Only if someone caught you. We'll stay by a stream."

I stepped forward, lifting her hand to my lips, and pressed a kiss to her knuckles. "Would that I could join you on this adventure, Lady, but the folk of lakes and streams depend on me to keep them safe. I can't risk their lives for a bit of merriment."

My chest pulled tight with the ache of wanting her to know how badly I wanted to follow—to rid myself of the responsibilities I was drowning in—to be free as she was. But this life, with its sacrifices, was one I could never relinquish. My parents' death assured that.

Sav's gaze dipped to her hand in mine, and she tugged it free, as she always did, and turned around, staring across the stream that separated Spring and Summer. Some time in the past few decades, Prince Fero had erected a wall of SnapDragons behind the natural border, an extra layer of defense, more against my spies than the prince of Spring, I thought. While Alder Hawthorn was a vicious tyrant to his folk, he rarely troubled himself with anything outside his court.

Or, it may have been Winter he protected his borders against as they rivaled each other for land on the continent and shared the longest border. But what land fae would need to protect themself from the queen?

5

Sav glanced back at me before staring longingly over the border once more. She was a free spirit, and it was that very spirit that had captured my heart. A heart that wasn't meant to beat for any creature—especially not the land fae standing with me now.

"Sav!"

We turned in unison, searching the copse of trees for a sign of the owner of the voice.

"Sav Briar! Get back here at once or Father will skin your hide."

Sav rolled her eyes, balancing on the balls of her feet. "I'm going. Stay here if you won't come with me."

Not waiting for my reply, she leaped over the wall of SnapDragons and disappeared into the thick foliage of Summer's forest.

"Savvvvvv!" Sage yelled again, crashing to a halt several yards from me. Sav's twin glanced down, smoothing her skirts. "Prince Kaspar. What brings you to our woods?"

Her voice was syrupy sweet, an act she'd recently begun putting on for me. I didn't blame her for wanting to find a way out of her impending marriage, but I couldn't save her from her fate.

"Lady Briar, good to see you." I dipped my chin in a show of deference to the role she would soon assume. "I am merely ensuring my streams flow true to the sea with no nefarious impediments."

"Surely you can't think—"

"Of course not, Lady. Your future husband is an honorable male." I cut her off. The words couldn't be further from the truth, but a reminder that I was very aware of her upcoming nuptials made her bite her lip. "But Summer's honor has always been... seasonal."

Sage closed the distance between us, raising a hand to accept the kiss I hadn't offered. I obliged, wrapping my fingers around her smooth skin. As my lips pressed against her knuckles, soft from years indoors, I thought of Sav's. She spent her days climbing trees and rocks, throwing knives and collecting rare herbs. Her hands told a story of the life she lived despite their parents. Sage, though nearly identical in appearance, was wholly different from her twin.

SPRING

"Would you care to walk with me?" Sage batted her lashes, and I wanted to laugh, but laughing was not a thing water fae did. Dipping my chin, I ushered her forward, not turning to spare another glance for the creature who had disappeared into the forest with my heart.

CHAPTER 2

Sav

I gripped the knife and pressed flat against the stone wall, heart pounding. Sage had, no doubt, come to drag me to another dress fitting or meeting with a court-appointed official. She was the one getting married, but it seemed I would be required to attend all the same etiquette lessons to ensure our family's low standing didn't tarnish the Hawthorn reputation by association.

High tinkling laughter disrupted the humid breeze, fraying my already strained nerves. I wiped a hand over my brow, exhaling the hot air that had only seemed to intensify the farther into Summer I went. Rumors of the prince's immense power stretched across Faerie, and I longed for a look at the male everyone simultaneously feared and desired.

When Sage took her place by Alder's side, I would be there as well, a pretty decoration to be bartered and traded at Father's leisure. He'd mentioned to Uncle on more than one occasion that Prince Fero was the ultimate catch, and I knew I would be flung at him when the moment presented itself. Better to see the male I'd be offered to before they wrapped a bow around my wrists.

A marriage between two courts could only be achieved through Mab's blessing, and those were so rare I hadn't heard of one in my lifetime, but my family cared only for the power I could wield if I landed in his bed. A prince was a prince after all. Should he ever take a wife, my family would expect me to ensure a place by his side at whatever cost. Or my uncle would at least.

Father didn't bother with much now that Mother was gone. A twinge of guilt twisted my gut. I should mourn her death as he did, but his sadness was enough to drown Faerie, and I feared there were no tears left for the rest of us.

Tanned legs skipped along the sandy bank that made up one side of Summer's castle, and I ducked low. A female, bare except for her chiming ankle bracelet, ran into the surf laughing and screaming as waves of bright aquamarine crashed against her skin. Her breasts floated in the sparkling water as she sank lower, and I ran a hand over my tightly restrained chest, wondering if the water could strip me bare too.

Though Spring had its own coastline, it was all rocky, jutting edges and a frigid ocean. Nothing like the warm sea air tickling my nose in Summer.

A male with the same tanned skin and raven hair waded into the water, chuckling as he reached the female bobbing with the waves. He wrapped his arms around her, pulling her flush to him and dipped his head, sucking one of her bronzed buds into his mouth. She let out a delighted laugh, and I leaned forward, eyes raking over her form as he licked and sucked her breasts.

Heat crept down my neck, and my nipples peaked, straining against the confines of my corset. What would it be like to know a man so intimately? To feel his tongue on my heated skin? My one and only encounter had been nothing like this.

The female rested her arms atop his broad shoulders and wrapped her legs around his waist. In the sparkling translucent water, nothing was hidden from view, and my mouth fell open when she moved swiftly, forcing herself down on his erection. He gripped her hips tightly as he guided her body.

Tension coiled low in my belly, and I froze in place, heat scorching my thighs as the couple moaned loudly, biting and sucking each other.

"Hasn't anyone ever told you it's impolite to intrude on a private moment?"

I spun and found a mountain of a male looming over me, his bronze skin in stark contrast with his raven hair. I stumbled backward, heart in my throat. I couldn't stop my eyes from drifting to the impressive length hanging between his legs, tangling my thoughts. I knew I should feel the danger of being caught in Summer, but all I could register was the way everything about this male seemed to press against my skin.

"What? I..." I bit my lip, backing up. My back pressed against the wall, but there was nowhere to go and the male was dangerously close. The heat creeping up my abdomen burned.

His lids narrowed, cutting orange irises, prominent in this court, to slits. "What are you doing in Summer?"

His words were casual—too casual. As if the answer didn't matter. He may have fooled a fae less accustomed to court politics, but I sensed his coaxing magic, and it ignited a flame in my veins. This male would not trick me, and who exactly did he think he was? Two could play his game.

Eyes wide, I mumbled: "I was lost and... so thirsty..."

The male raised an eyebrow, and his lips turned up at the corners. "By all means, allow me to escort you into the palace, where you may rest and receive aid."

That was dumb, Sav. I cleared my throat, straightening. "That won't be necessary. I'll find my way."

I pressed off the wall, attempting to dart around him, but his arm snaked out, thick fingers gripping my biceps roughly.

"Unhand me!" I demanded, all my earlier embarrassment evaporating, leaving only a spark of fury. Something hot crackled under my skin, and for a heartbeat the edges of my vision blurred crimson.

He didn't release me. Even as I twisted in his hold, he only drew me back a step, and I stumbled forward, palm flattening against the ridged planes of his bare abdomen.

He hauled me upright, his eyes locking with mine, amusement glinting there. "If you want me to sate the hunger burning between your thighs, Lady, you need only ask."

Searing heat licked across my palm where I touched him, and I shoved hard, wrenching free of his grasp. "You are a foul, uncouth male, and I will not be spoken to that way." The fury inside me swelled, kindling into something wild and consuming, scorching me from within. My heart pounded against my ribs. What was happening to me?

He chuckled, oblivious to the panic clawing at me, but made no move to grab me again. Not waiting to see what he would do next, I backed up and turned, bolting from him and the summer castle. His deep, rumbling laugh followed as I fled.

I ran and ran, not slowing until I was safely in Ferndell village. At Ivy's vine-wrapped door, I pounded with shaking fists, desperate. "Ivy. Ivy, please."

It swung open, and Ivy, the town healer, stood, hand on her hip, glaring down at me. "What have you done now, Sav?"

I pushed past her, stepping inside. Her home was quaint, an oversized wooden table near the window taking up most of the room's space. I slid onto its smooth surface as I had many times before, but this time, I had no physical injury to show her. I held up my palms, and she came to stand beside me.

"There's something wrong with me. My hands are burning."

She narrowed her eyes, squinting at my outstretched palms. "I see nothing, Sav."

"You don't understand. I touched... something, and it felt like my palm was on fire and... my body was burning."

Ivy wiped a hand on her apron, leaving streaks of dirt behind. Her bright red locks gleamed in the sunlight, and several dozen freckles were stark against her pale skin. Where the specks dotting my checks and chest were barely noticeable against tanned skin, Ivy's fair complexion contrasted dramatically with hers. She was nearly covered in them. Even the tips of her pointed ears had a dusting of brown specks.

She lifted a finger to my outstretched palm and pressed the pad to my skin before yanking her hand back, hissing. "How far off is your birthday?"

I frowned. "It's nearly six months until I turn twenty-five. Why?" I hopped off the dining table that doubled as a patient's examination table. "Do you think it has to do with my magic?"

Ivy backed up, motioning for me to follow. I did, trailing her through a narrow hall. Stretching up the walls, flora in shades of white, blue, and fuchsia stretched toward me, reminding me of the wall of blooms at the castle on a much smaller scale. Buds burst into full bloom, some shriveling back moments later.

Her mouth turned down, and she glanced between me and the blooms. "Sav, you're a Leo, correct?"

I nodded.

Her pursed lips and furrowed brow sent a bolt of ice through me. "What is it?"

"Nothing." She paced away from me.

I trailed after, and the flora along her wall strained against their vines to follow. I eyed them warily. "Tell me."

"Your sister's wedding is in less than three months."

I bit my lip. I didn't need a reminder. It was all that occupied my family's minds. She'd planned a visit to the Lady of the Lake's restorative waters. New jewels. New shoes. The list of preparations was endless. I understood, of course. We were not royal. If Sage hoped to be accepted by our court, she would have to look the part of a princess.

"Would you agree to a bargain?"

I looked up, meeting Ivy's hazel eyes. They were dull by fae standards, but I'd never asked her about it. It was impolite to ask a fae about the brightness of their eyes. "What sort of bargain?"

"Come help me here for the next few months and promise not to go to the castle until after your sister is wed. In exchange, I'll offer you a place here when she is married."

I wrinkled my nose. "Why?"

She eyed me for a long moment, seeming to come to some decision. "I believe life at court would be dangerous for you. Better you find work elsewhere. You have a knack for herbs, and I could use the help."

I backed up, inching toward the door. The thought of staying with Ivy nestled in my chest, but my mother would reach through the veil to strangle me herself if I accepted such a position. Not to mention, my sister would be Princess of Spring. The sister of a princess could not become a healer's assistant.

"My father would never agree." I reached behind me, feeling for the door. "I had better go. They'll be wondering where I am."

"Wait!" Ivy flung her hands out, and the handle froze.

I wriggled it, but it was stuck tight. My heart sped up. "Ivy?"

She stepped closer, palms stretched toward me. "Sav, please listen. I want only what's best for you."

"Why did you lock me in?"

"You must know how dangerous it could be for your family if anyone believed you were more powerful than Sage.

A laugh sputtered from my lips. "More... powerful? Than Sage? She's the greatest earth fae of our time."

"I hope that's true."

My stomach did a somersault, and I gripped the handle at my back tighter. "I'm not a Virgo. Please, Ivy. You're scaring me." Heat crept down my skin as she inched toward me, as if I were a spooked deer.

"Your births were so close together. What if they got it wrong? What if *you* were the fae meant to lead Spring?"

No, it wasn't true. And no male would tether me to a role that demanded subservience, especially not Alder Hawthorn. A memory of Alder's sweat-slick fingers sliding down my neck, brushing my hair aside as he inhaled my scent, rocked through me, and I shook my head as the room tinted red. Ivy's eyes went wide, and she backed up. "Sav?"

His dry lips brushed the vein pulsing at my throat as he murmured in my ear. "A flower in bloom." I shook my head again, trying to rid myself of the memory as the heat burned a path up my spine. It boiled in my veins, threatening to char me from the inside. I expelled a breath, and a plume of white smoke escaped my nostrils.

Ivy backed up, glancing behind her. "Sav, calm down."

His lips trailed south, but I was frozen. He was the prince. To deny him meant death. Bile burned in my throat at the thought of giving my body to him. Heat scalded my back, burning the base of my spine, and flames raced along my skin. Bindings—cinching me in tightly—caught fire, disintegrating to ash, and I inhaled a deep breath for the first time since donning this dress today. The vined door behind me squealed and creaked, and the handle bent under my flaming grip.

Ivy took another step back, and a hot tear ran down my cheek.

"What's happening?" I begged.

Metal melted in my palm, and I stumbled backward, landing on my butt in the dirt outside Ivy's home. Agony split me in half, and when I screamed, it wasn't sound that came out, it was fire. A torrent of it, like my soul had torn open. I cupped a hand over my lips. My gaze darted around the deserted town as I climbed to my feet.

A memory danced in my mind, of Sage bursting in to find her betrothed pressing kisses against my clammy skin; her shrill cries as she flung accusations at me for tricking him into believing I was her. Red sparks erupted from my fingertips, and I backed away from Ivy's home, but I wasn't fast enough. The raging, burning inferno lodged in my throat burst free, and a wildfire exploded from my mouth, my hands, my chest. It whipped out, catching what remained of Ivy's door, setting her front step, the walls, the roof, ablaze.

The sky was black in moments, and I spun away from her home. The fire didn't stop. It raged. It consumed me and everything in its wake.

Leaving Ferndell, I raced through the forest, letting out small whimpers as sparks caught on the branches stretching toward me, attempting to comfort me. I reached the edge of the lake and dove in, desperate to drown the memories along with the flames.

The shock of cold water doused my raging fire. I opened my eyes, blinking as the world slowly returned to a cool shade of blue. Around me, sea folk scattered, darting away, and I spared a moment's concern for what it might mean if they knew my truth.

As the chill sunk in, I relaxed, puzzling over the implications of this new revelation. I was not an earth sign, as Ivy feared, but my power had come early, and it had come with a force I'd scarcely heard described in legend. A fae gained their magic on their twenty-fifth birthday, but it was a trickle—an inkling of what was to come.

What did it mean that mine arrived so early, so strong? And what would it destroy next?

CHAPTER 3

Kaspar

A shockwave tore through the walls of my castle, shaking stones loose and sending folk scuttling in every direction. An attack. Someone dared strike my court. I swam for the door, yanking my knives from their sheath, catching the current pulsing in my veins and harnessing it to carry me to the shore. To one of the three borders I shared with Spring.

I slowed as the water warmed, but no other shockwave came. Whatever had detonated in my underwater court, it had not repeated. Folk and fish swam past me, eyes wide as they escaped whatever had just exploded. I continued on, pressing my fingers out to form a protective shield around me.

In the distance, deep red, like high fae blood, carried on the current, and I moved faster.

A figure drifted into view through the settling haze, a land fae, wrapped in the charred remains of what had once been an emerald gown.

"Sav!" I sheathed my knives.

I raced for her, catching her limp form in my arms and carrying her to the surface. We broke through, and she inhaled a sharp breath. Bright violet eyes sparkled in the afternoon sun as they met mine.

"Sav. Are you injured?" My gaze traveled the length of her, searching for the cause of her dazed expression; her blackened clothing. No blood. No burns. Just scorched fabric and a tangle of auburn hair wrapped around her like seaweed.

Swimming for the pebbled beach, I pressed her feverish skin against mine, hoping it would cool her. When we reached land, my tail split, forming legs, and I strode for her home, wrapping my arms tightly around her.

"No," she breathed.

I glanced down, continuing forward. "You'll be well when I get you home."

"No," she protested—more forcefully this time. "Ivy."

Yes. Of course. The healer would know what to do. Sav's eyes rolled back in her head before falling closed and I stretched my legs, speeding up as I cradled her to me. My cold heart thundered a strange, unwanted rhythm as I surged forward.

Whoever had done this to Sav drew their last breath today.

I reached Ferndell and stopped. My jaw tightened as I took in the scene. Flames licked up blackened rooftops, folk dashing to a fro, putting out the remnants of what must have been a raging blaze. *Summer.* They'd caught Sav and retaliated. It was the only answer. I'd made a promise to myself—for my folk—that I would find peace with Summer, but if he had attacked Spring, attacked Sav, he was dead.

I found the healer's home, or what remained of it, still burning, and turned in a slow circle. No one paid me any mind as they worked quickly. The healer's bright hair wasn't among the fae working to put out the fire. "Ivy! Your subject needs aid!"

Flaming curls burst through the door to my left and raced forward. "Bring her. Quickly." She darted to a stone bench behind her smoking home, the only space that wasn't blackened, and waited for me to set Sav down.

Cradling her head gently, I laid her body atop the slab.

Ivy leaned over Sav, peeling an eyelid back. "Did you drench her?" She looked up at me. "To put out her flame?"

I swallowed. Her flame? *Her* flame. Had *she* rocked my castle? But it was too soon. She had not yet reached a quarter of a century, and land fae didn't gain their magic until twenty-five. "I found her in my lake."

Ivy's pink lips formed an o, and her eyes widened. She dipped low. "I beg your pardon, Your Highness. I did not recognize you."

"Stand. Attend your patient." I growled. I inhaled sharply, processing this new information. *Sav caused this destruction*. She had come into her magic early and set this small village alight. What had been the catalyst to spark her magic so many months before her birthday? Magic this early, this violent—if her father learned of it, he'd barter her at court. And every noble would want her in his pocket.

Sav's eyelids fluttered, and I moved, leaning to inspect her face. Her breath came shallow, her skin leached of color, but no wounds marred her flesh. Burnout, no doubt. For her first time, magic of this scale would have devoured her. It must have been building for weeks. Preparing to be discharged. She likely wouldn't have survived if she'd waited till her birthday to release it.

"Kaspar?"

My name, whispered on soft lips, had my whole being straining toward her, and I knelt on one knee, dipping my head to hers, ignoring Ivy's gasp.

"Yes, Princess?"

She rasped a laugh, her throat still raw from the magic that had burned its way free. "I'm no princess."

"To me, you are royalty."

She blinked, and her eyes met the fae's behind me.

Ivy hovered insufferably close, pressing her warmth into my back. I leaned toward Sav. Another might have been drawn and quartered for the impertinence, but the only thing that mattered now was Sav's recovery.

"Sav, can you hear me?" the healer asked.

Sav nodded, holding out a hand. I knocked Ivy's outstretched palm aside, wrapping my fingers around hers to gently help her up. She sat, gaze going in and out of focus as she took in the damage her magic had caused.

A sob caught in her throat. "Did I... do all this?"

Ivy spoke, but I blocked her view, leaning closer so Sav saw only me. "You are magnificent. Your gift will rival any land fae's. Do not apologize for having power."

Sav snorted a laugh, and I heard Ivy mutter something about repairing her home under her breath as I stood and pulled Sav to her feet. She glanced around, cheeks staining red. "Please forgive me, Ivy."

"I'll see it's repaired," I said, cutting off another of Ivy's inane comments. "Your only concern should be recovering."

"I should go home."

I nodded, but Ivy cleared her throat. "She cannot return to her family in this state. They must not know."

My hold tightened on Sav's. The healer was right. I hadn't considered it, but Sav's family was hungry for power. If they knew the magic she possessed, they would exploit it. "Princess, you must change first."

Sav frowned. "Don't call me that."

I smiled. "As my lady wishes."

Her lips lifted at the corners, but she grimaced after a moment. "Get Sage. Ask her to bring me a dress."

"I don't think—" Ivy began.

"We can trust her, Ivy." Sav cut her off.

Ivy bit down hard on a reply. I was inclined to agree with the healer in this instance. Sage was nothing if not petty and jealous. If she knew her sister's magic had come early, there was no telling what she would do.

"I will ask her. Stay with Ivy and let no one see you in this state."

Sav turned round violet eyes on me, and the trust in her gaze nearly broke me. To have that look, to hold it in my heart, would sustain me in all the cold months I would spend underwater until I saw her next.

I released her hand, cooler now than it had been when I found her in the water, and turned to leave.

"Kaspar?"

I twisted back.

"Thank you."

My brow dipped into a deep V. "Never give your thanks."

"I mean it. Name your favor, and you shall have it."

My lips tipped into a lazy grin as I turned away to find her sister. I would not request a favor of my princess today, but one day, when the moment was right, I would ask something of her she could not refuse, and when I did, she would be mine forever.

CHAPTER 4

Sav

I n my room, in Sage's borrowed gown, I leaned against my door, exhaling a long sigh. Kaspar had worked his silver-tongued magic on my sister, and she'd sent him with one of her plainer dresses. It was tight. She had always been slimmer than me—less muscular—but when I loosened the stays, it just barely fit.

"Sav?"

Sage's tentative voice through the door gave me pause.

I pushed off the wood, tugging it open, and stared at my twin. Her eyes were round, and my heart lurched at the terror on her face. "Come in."

She swished billowing skirts into the room and closed the door behind her.

I held out my hands, and she took them, squeezing too hard. Her amethyst eyes locked on mine, wide and glassy with unshed tears.

"I'm scared," she whispered, voice shaking. "Not of the ball... Of what comes after."

I squeezed back. "Sage..."

"What if he changes his mind?" She pulled back, folding her arms across her chest like armor. "What if I'm not as powerful as the lady predicted?"

A shard of ice lodged in my chest, but I swallowed it down and brushed a strand of hair from her face, swiping the faint freckles on her cheek. "You'll be everything she foresaw and more. Brave, beautiful, and stronger than you know. Any male would be lucky to have you."

Sage's shoulders relaxed a fraction, and her lips tipped up in a trembling smile. "Do you think he'll ask me?"

"Sage, it's done. Tonight is only a formality."

I tried to sound confident, but memories of the night Alder had dragged me from the dance floor and only my sister had stopped him from taking what he wanted, lived dangerously close to the surface, threatening to boil over again. Heat sizzled in my veins, but I swallowed it down.

She nodded, smoothing silk over her thighs. "Promise you'll come with me when I move into the palace." She looked up, spearing me with an accusatory stare.

Inhaling a calming breath, I attempted to slow my thrumming pulse. I wanted to be there for my sister, but Ivy's warning—the magic I wasn't supposed to have—and memories of Alder's advances crept in, making my palms slick. I wiped my hands down the pale fabric of my sister's borrowed gown. She wouldn't move in yet. We had several weeks before she was expected at court, and I could make excuses to come after. Offer to stay behind to pack her belongings; care for Father; delay.

"Sav. Please. I need you. You're all I have."

Her words pierced my chest, and I nodded slowly. If our roles had been reversed, I would have made the same desperate request. I would have needed my sister.

"Of course."

Sage cleared her throat and stood, staring down imperiously. "You can't go to the ball like that. Bathe and, for Mab's sake, wear something pretty. We're to be royalty, and a royal doesn't dress like a peasant." She swept from the room, confidence restored, and I fell back on my bed, gazing up at the twining vines woven overhead.

Time to make myself presentable for court.

As we approached Spring's castle, I couldn't help but compare its size with the sandstone monolith that was Summer's palace. Where our court's palace was a stone fortress, overgrown with ivy and thorns, set amidst a lush garden of blooming flowers, Summer's sprawling estate sat on sandy shores that backed up to a glittering aquamarine beach.

There were no high walls or glass windows; only endless pillars and stretches of open courtyard. It spoke of how little rain they received. How free might my life have been in a principality with none of the confines of Spring's rigid traditions and court politics?

Sage looped her arm through mine, and we stepped into the grand hall. She squeezed as a bouquet bloomed, stretching toward us. My stomach flipped, but when I glanced at Sage, her eyes were alight with wonder. She held out her hand, running the pads of her fingers over the delicate petals.

I shuddered, leaning toward her. The ones closest to us wilted, peeling back and drifting lazily to the floor. Sage snatched her fingers back, tugging me forward. Her heart raced, and I longed to tell her it wasn't *her* magic scalding the flora. But to admit that would mean telling her everything, and tonight was her night. My troubles could wait.

At the end of the long hall, massive arched doors stretched wide, and we stepped through. My head tipped back as I took in the ballroom's splendor. Far overhead, vines wove together, and bouquets of wildflowers dotted the spired ceiling in faelight, illuminating the space. In small cages, pixies danced to the music, dusting glitter over revelers. The air was thick with the scent of lilac, rose, and honeysuckle.

We had been to court many times but had never been invited to a royal ball, until now.

Sage's birth had been auspicious, and the Lady of the Lake, a creature of great power and eminence, had deigned to set foot on land to proclaim her our next princess. Yet even with her proclamation, the Hawthorn family had waited until Sage was nearly of age to announce her ascension.

I'd overheard Uncle Robin confess to Father the royals had secretly hoped another would be born before she could claim her place, but in twenty-four years, no other Virgos rivaled what was expected to be the greatest gift Spring had known in a thousand years. The Hawthorns relied entirely on their brides for power. Although they had wed the strongest earth fae with each union, their sons were never born with even a flicker of earth magic.

Each court uniquely selected its ruler, and in ours, it seemed a noble would always be forced to marry a commoner to ensure the principality remained stable. Winter only ever had one queen. Unlike the rest of us, Mab was eternal. Autumn relied on their seers to prophecise the next prince or princess, and Summer chose their ruler by power alone.

We reached the foot of twin thrones and bowed low, not yet considered members of the royal court.

"Rise," Prince Hawthorn commanded in a bored voice.

My gaze snagged on the male seated beside Alder. Prince Foxglove. He was sharper, his features as elegant as they were unreadable. An unsettling pressure crept behind my eyes, like fingers brushing against my thoughts. I looked away, throat tightening.

Beside me, Sage swayed. Alder hadn't even looked at her.

I gripped her arm, steadying her, and forced myself to meet Alder's gaze. He lounged on his throne, head tilted, attention drifting lazily over the ballroom—everywhere but on us.

Look at her. I silently willed him. *Let her feel chosen, just once.*

But Alder was making a point.

Seconds passed. I could feel my sister's confidence fraying.

Then Foxglove leaned in, his lips barely moving. A whisper.

Alder's eyes snapped back. Not to Sage—but to me.

He let his gaze drag over me, from the points of my ears to my collarbone, and then flicked his fingers in dismissal. "Go. Enjoy yourselves. But do not overindulge."

Heat rose in my veins as we were dismissed, and Sage turned us around. We stopped at a low table, and I exhaled a slow breath to calm the irrational urge to go back and fling my dagger at the tender place between his thighs he left so carelessly unguarded.

"He seemed pleased to see me," Sage gushed, swiping a glass of henbane wine from the long table set along the wall of the ballroom. My sister was no fool. That she chose to interpret anything about that moment in a positive light spoke of her nerves. She reached for a second glass, handing it to me. "Drink this. You're stiff as a board."

I glowered at her but lifted the cup to my lips. Perhaps she was right. A drink would dull my senses and cool my temper. A repeat of earlier today would be disastrous.

"Ladies."

Kaspar's voice cut through my fury. I spun, grin already spreading, as I found him there, every inch the prince of Lakes and Streams in shades of navy and teal, turquoise eyes alight with mischief.

Sage dipped her chin, assuming the role of princess before she even had the title, but I released her arm and grabbed Kaspar's.

"Sav," she hissed. "That's—"

I ignored her, tugging Kaspar with me onto the dance floor.

"I'm so glad you're here," I whispered just above the music.

He wrapped an arm around my waist, and we launched into motion. Cool fingers traced a circle on my back, calming my nerves, and soon the simmering heat in my veins was a distant memory. He was taller than me like this, just enough to make me tilt my head back, but I'd seen the shape he could take. In Kelpie form, he was a stunning creature who towered over us all and commanded his court with the even temper of a sea fae.

And yet... he never pressed the weight of his magic against me the way other royals did. Their power suffocated. His presence steadied. Perhaps that was why, with Kaspar, I felt safe.

He had not come to rescue me though. Tonight, he represented Lakes and Streams. As ally to the spring court, he was here to bear witness to my sister's formal betrothal. On this night, a prince or princess attended for one of two reasons. To acknowledge the union or object to it.

Kaspar would never do such a thing to one of his dearest friends, but the autumn prince would soon arrive, and Uncle speculated Summer might make an appearance as well. Either ruler could speak against the marriage if they had cause. Mab would not attend. She didn't trouble herself with fae court politics, leaving us to squabble amongst ourselves.

General Creig, commander of Spring's guard, stalked into the room, and my gaze locked on his tall frame as he pushed through the crowd, marching to the throne. We had only met once—nearly a decade ago—and I dearly hoped he didn't remember the encounter. I stumbled when I caught sight of the male trailing behind him. Kaspar's gaze drifted from mine to see what had captured my attention, and he stiffened.

"Let us find refreshment," he said, leading me from the dance floor.

I moved dumbly, following him, but never lost sight of the broad frame of a raven-haired male in Summer Court finery. Though he'd been naked the last time I laid eyes on him, there was no mistaking his wide shoulders or the piercing orange orbs that swept over the room, landing on me.

Mab take me. It wasn't just any fae who had found me outside the palace this morning.

Creig cleared his voice, and even from this distance, the introduction was clear. "Presenting Prince Fero of the summer court."

His focus returned to the throne, and he gave an infinitesimal dip of his chin to Prince Alder. Foxglove had disappeared, and Alder sat up straighter, dropping his head low. A smile crept onto my face, and I reveled in his discomfort; in seeing him reminded of the weak power coursing through his veins. He recovered quickly, welcoming the prince to our court and sweeping an arm in a wide arc. "Please drink, eat, and find comfort in whomever you choose as your companion this night."

The grin slid from my lips. Of course Alder would offer the entirety of his folk to a foreign prince to be used for his pleasure. We belonged to him—chattel to be sold and traded.

Prince Fero replied, but his words were drowned in the next swell of music, and Kaspar's cool palm found my arm, twisting me around to face him. Seafoam eyes scoured me, searching for the cause of my discomfort.

"Do not fear the male. Tonight, you're with me."

I laughed, gaze dropping. "Be serious, Kaspar. You are a prince, and I am a commoner."

His fingers touched my chin, tipping it up. "To me, you will always be a princess."

"Fine words. Will there be two betrothals this evening?"

I spun at the clipped voice, its mockery slicing down my spine like ice.

Prince Fero's sharp gaze darted to Kaspar's arm, still gripping my biceps, and swept slowly over my friend. When his eyes met mine, his lips tipped up, and I froze. He was every bit the lethal ruler I'd heard he was, and he knew my secret. He could do anything to me for trespassing on his land. Though I was a commoner now, in a matter of hours, I would be something more, and he might use my actions to wage war on Spring.

Suddenly, I understood Kaspar's refusal earlier in the day. Understood what was at stake for my court because of me.

"If she's not yet spoken for, I request the pleasure of a dance."

Kaspar moved to stand in front of me, but I tugged my arm from his hold and turned to face him. "I will return. Find Sage. Make sure she's well."

Kaspar stared impassively back at me, and for a moment, I wished he shared any of the land fae's emotions, but perhaps it was a good thing he did not. I was certain another fae would have caused a scene.

Turning to Prince Fero, I slipped my hand in his and let him lead me away.

He was tall, and I strained my neck to stare up at him, but though he was a massive brute of a fae, he was a competent dancer, and in moments, I was lost to the music; carried on the magic swelling through the room.

"I must admit, I didn't expect to find you at court tonight."

My brow furrowed. "Do you know me?"

He barked a laugh, and several fae spinning around us glanced our way.

His large fingers tightened over mine, and he tugged me closer as we continued to spin. The memory of his naked form towering over me as I spied on an intimate moment flashed through my mind, and heat stained my cheeks.

"After the day we've had together, I feel we can call each other old friends."

Embarrassment deepened, and I chastised myself for asking such a question. Of course he knew me. Glancing up at burning orange orbs, I noticed a small silver ball glinting in the faelight. It was a simple nose ring, but it was out of place on the face of a prince. He wore no other jewelry or adornments. No crown or gold atop his pointed ears. Apart from the finely woven cream fabric with bronze accents stretched over his shoulders, he showed no signs of being royalty.

But Prince Fero was not born royal. No one in Summer was. They selected their royalty based on power alone. More than a century ago, he had been tested, and to date, no one had ever come close to rivaling his magic. I took some comfort in knowing he had once been a commoner like me.

"Can I rely on my friend to keep my secret?" I asked.

He laughed again, a deep rumbling sound that made my lips tip up. Perhaps he wasn't as fearsome as our court claimed.

"Tell me then, new friend. What is your name?"

All mirth within me died as his power clawed its way down my throat, coiling around my name like a noose. I gagged, my true first name ripping free before I could stop it.

No. No. No.

SPRING

My heart stuttered—then thundered. He had it. My first name. Not just the one I used but the one that bound me. What could he do to me? What would he ask me to do for him? How could I fight him now?

I yanked my hand from his, stumbled back, crashing into velvet sleeves and murmured complaints. My throat burned. My skin itched. I needed to get away—needed air.

"Sav!" Kaspar called behind me, but I didn't look, didn't wait for him to come find me.

I pushed the doors wide and ran.

CHAPTER 5

Kaspar

S av raced from the ball, and several folk stared after her, casting wary glances at the prince of Summer. A low growl rumbled in my chest. After finding her in my lake earlier, I'd assumed she never made it to Summer's court. Assumed she had returned to the healer she gathered herbs for.

I hadn't learned what had caused her magic to erupt. Seeing the prince reminded me of my first inclination. Perhaps she had gone into Summer after all.

Murmurs grew louder as the prince she'd left standing awkwardly on the dance floor stalked from the room in the same direction as Sav. I pivoted on my toes. I was expected to play the calm and collected prince tonight. To indulge in wine and conversation with the eligible ladies of court, but I wanted nothing more than to go after them and ensure he didn't lay a hand on her.

Sage appeared beside me, and I ground my teeth, snatching a glass of dark liquid from the table at my side.

"Will you dance with me?"

30

She was as obvious as she was overdressed, but I couldn't refuse the future queen. It would cause a scandal that may have real consequences for her prospects tonight. She didn't know it, but Alder had made a desperate bid for a lady in Autumn. A slap in the face to Spring. The fae wasn't even a Virgo, but she *did* possess earth magic.

The Lady of the Lake might enact any form of retribution if he went through with it, and that would effectively sever ties between our two courts. Though the Lady was no member of my court, her wild fae magic was bound to my court, and her actions would be a direct reflection on me. I had no desire to be at war with my closest neighbor.

There was, of course, still the matter of Mab's consent, but my spies reported that Alder had reason to believe his request would be granted. Some dark secret his family knew that could be used to grant them favors. If there were any truth to it, I would find out.

I held out a hand, and Sage took it. Her pulse raced, and I ran my thumb over the jumping veins in her wrist, tugging her onto the dance floor. She looked up, bright eyes meeting mine, and for a moment I could almost imagine it was Sav looking at me like she needed rescuing.

But Sav would never look at me that way. At anyone that way.

Wrapping an arm around Sage's waist, I led her confidently through a formal dance, keeping a respectful distance. It wouldn't have raised Alder's jealousy, but I had no doubt my show of support was all the reminder he needed that I was firmly on the side of my Lady of the Lake's choice in princess.

Sage inched closer as we spun, pressing her chest against mine, and I held back the urge to roll my eyes. She would be powerful—the Lady of the Lake had predicted it, and she was never wrong—but her insecurities made her weak in other ways. Ways that could be exploited. I feared what a princess who could be so easily manipulated would mean for the future of our alliance.

"You look delectable tonight, Sage." I bit the inside of my cheek to hide my grimace. Sage's ego was easily fed and she would need that confidence tonight.

She batted her lashes, pressing closer and dipped back, sliding herself seductively up my body as we passed the throne, and I gave her a lazy smile. She glanced over a shoulder, catching her betrothed watching us, and her lips tipped up.

"You're handsome as ever, Prince Kaspar." She glanced back again.

"Don't look at him. Look at me." Her confidence faltered, and she missed the next step. I tightened my hold on her, guiding her through the movements. "If you make it obvious, he won't take the bait."

Sage's nails bit into my palm as she squeezed my hand, but her expression smoothed into one of a regal lady, and she found her footing, regaining the rhythm. Soon we were dipping and gliding through the steps, her future husband forgotten.

"May I cut in?" Alder's nasal voice scraped against my ears, but I loosened my grip, stepping back, and Sage betrayed only a moment's hesitation before she accepted his hand and they were swept away by the song.

Shaking out my fingers to regain some of the feeling, I strode quickly through the room. Sav hadn't returned, and neither had the prince, and though I knew she could hold her own, even against a prince, I didn't trust him.

Following the carefully laid path along the gardens outside the palace, my gaze slid over manicured lawns and boxed hedges, noting the glittering golden jays sparkling in the moonlight and lending a soft glow to the path. Like the halls of Spring's castle, the hedges were a maze, and even with no princess on the throne, magic swelled through the gardens, and flora swayed to the music.

A laugh caught my ear, and my gaze swiveled to the tallest hedges obscuring the center of the maze. Sav laughed again, and I moved faster, twisting and turning, dodging the lovely poison-tipped blooms stretching for me. Though their tips weren't lethal, they were intended to give revelers a strong high that would have muddled my senses. I needed a clear head to face the prince of Summer.

I rounded the last corner as one of the golden jays took flight, taking its light with it and my heart beat against my chest. Would I find them in some compromising position? His lips pressed to her fevered skin, his fingers brushing feather-light over the outline of her peaked nipples? I could handle dalliances, trysts in the darkened corners of the garden, but a prince with so much more to offer. Never.

I halted, blinking at the scene before me.

Sav looked up, face alight with glee. "Kaspar! You found us!"

She staggered to her feet, clutching a wine bottle like a lifeline before taking a swig. She'd been gone less than half an hour, yet managed to inebriate herself. My gaze slid to the fae at her side. Sav had fled the ball empty-handed, but now she carried the very thing certain to loosen her tongue.

The fae, dressed in Spring Court finery, grinned coyly as Sav leaned into her arm for balance, a smile tugging at her lips.

"You're welcome," Sav slurred, and I bit back a laugh. For all my unease at finding her this way, she was damnably charming when she overindulged.

"Who is welcome, and to what, Lady?"

She blinked at me, then burst into laughter. "You're funny, Kaspar."

The spring court fae's gaze raked over me, her violet eyes glittering with amusement. "Kaspar. A pleasure."

I stiffened, reining in my temper. "I am Prince Kaspar, of Lakes and Streams. And you are?"

She dipped low, eyes falling to the grass at her feet. "I am Lady Primrose of House Magnolia. Second cousin to Prince Hawthorn of Spring."

Alarm bells rang in my head. A cousin of the prince of Spring—a female cousin—could be a dangerous foe. "Rise, Lady."

She did, her arm never wavering as Sav wobbled drunkenly at her side. Her lilac eyes met mine, dull by fae standards, and they spoke of the curse that afflicted the royal line. I hadn't known it stretched to more distant relatives, but one look at her lackluster irises and it was clear whatever magic she had was a speck when compared with mine or the female at her side.

I arched a brow, searching her face. "What brings a pair of females out to the gardens after dark when a ball is underway?" Had Sav been sober, she would have leveled me with one of her famous glares or perhaps thrown something at me, but in her current state, I wasn't sure she'd heard me at all.

"I was in need of a companion. The ball was stifling; too many male egos for such a small space." Lady Primrose gave me a sly smile as if she expected me to collude with her, but my gaze slid to Sav who had burst into another fit of giggles.

The hair on my arms prickled. Primrose was too poised. Too sober. Her smiles too carefully measured. There was something very wrong with this situation. She glanced at Sav, whose eyes were struggling to remain open. She leaned into her sober companion, mumbling something incoherent.

"It appears Lady Briar needs an escort. Allow me to offer you both an arm."

Lady Primrose smiled demurely, taking my arm. Sav swayed, nearly toppling to the ground, and I caught her just before she could go down. She blinked up at me, dazed, the fire usually crackling behind her gaze reduced to embers. A tightness gripped my chest.

What had Fero done?

She barely seemed to register me as I propped her against my hip. When I looked up, Lady Primrose was eyeing me with interest.

In that moment, I understood what she had contrived, and I had been a willing participant in her game. But I had never made my acquaintance with Sav a secret, and I wouldn't start now. I stepped onto the path, leading my companions back toward the castle. Sav stumbled, tripping over every root and branch in her path. Lady Primrose's gaze slid to me again, calculating. The chill down my spine had nothing to do with the evening air.

What if it wasn't my relationship to Sav she wanted to ferret out, but my emotion for her? Was Hawthorn's cousin testing my weakness—or my heart?

And if she was working for someone with secrets about Mab...

I might've just handed them exactly what they needed.

CHAPTER 6

Sav

I flopped heavily onto the grand bed laid out for my stay in the castle and groaned. My heartbeat pulsed against my skull, begging to be freed of bone and flesh, blood pounding in my ears.

"I'll fetch water." Kaspar's voice was a faint whisper, barely audible over the drumbeat rattling my brain. I tried to tell him not to worry about it, to let me rest in peace, in the dark, quiet of my temporary room, but he slipped out the door and was gone before I opened my mouth.

Fuzzy memories of the night flitted through my mind, murky and hard to grasp. I had danced with Prince Fero, then I was in the garden, but I couldn't remember why. Hiding or... had to get out... It was hovering just out of reach. Then Primrose had appeared, bottle in hand, complaining of a male whose roving hands made her want to stab something, and I'd known at once we were kindred spirits.

"You were dancing with a prince," she said. "Two of them."

"Yes." I pressed a hand against the shrub, reveling in the mindless euphoria the tiny tips of its white blossoms brought. I couldn't remember why I had wanted that escape.

36

She had handed me the bottle after taking a swig. "Males. They think they own us. Princes are no better than the rest." She had smiled at me, and I felt it—a truly kindred spirit.

"I'm Sav."

"Primrose."

A light knock came at my door. I tried to sit up, but the slightest movement made the room tilt and my head dropped onto the pillow. "Enter."

Kaspar's calming presence followed him in and the bed dipped. Cool fingers slid under my neck, lifting my head toward a bronze cup. A memory of bronze-edged sleeves holding my hand on the dance floor swam into focus in my mind.

I drank deeply, the liquid sliding down my throat in cooling waves. Its healing magic worked quickly, washing away some of the poison in my system, and the memory of my dance with Prince Fero sharpened. Something had happened. Something that made me risk angering a prince by leaving him on the dance floor. But what?

"A little more," Kaspar urged.

I swallowed the last drops of water and sat up, my vision clearing. I was by no means sober, but the poison was burning away quickly, and heat swelled in my veins to quell it, rising to aid me against any threat. And with it, a terrible certainty bloomed. Something had gone very, very wrong.

I blinked several times, gaze traveling to Kaspar beside me. I sat up. "What are you doing here? Someone could have seen you."

Kaspar pressed a cool palm to my forehead. "Relax, Princess. No one in the palace would question a prince visiting a female's chambers at night."

I leaned away. "They would if she was expected to marry. No noble would take me if they thought you'd laid a claim."

He tilted his head. "And what if I had?"

I stilled. "Kaspar—don't. I'm being serious."

His eyes searched mine for a beat too long. Then he cleared his throat and stood. "You're right. I shouldn't have come."

"Stop! Don't go. If you weren't seen before you might be now. You'll have to stay until the halls are clear."

Kaspar stood beside the bed, frozen, and for the first time in our friendship, I wondered if I had overstepped. He was a prince after all and likely had his own agenda for the evening. Alliances to forge, secrets to overhear, perhaps even a female's bed to attend. I had just commanded a prince. I looked up, eyes wide. "I didn't mean..."

He sat, giving me a small shove. "If you expect me to spend my time with a peasant, you could at least share some of this enormous bed."

I exhaled a laugh and scooted over. My magic continued burning away the henbane wine, and with each passing moment, my mind cleared. As it did, more of the evening came back to me, sliding out from behind a veil of muddled thoughts. I sat up gasping. Remembering why I had fled to the garden.

"Kaspar! He knows my name."

The words spilled out of me. My skin crawled, the memory of his power slithering through me like a parasite. Not just my name. My *true* name.

When I had recounted our conversation, the magic Prince Fero had used to extract my name and the piece of the night I hadn't remembered until now—when the magic in my veins had burned away his compulsion—I knew why I was drunk in the garden.

"He forced me to run my fingers over the petals in the maze so I wouldn't remember any of it."

Kaspar clasped my hands tightly as I fought down the urge to retch. I only remembered it because my magic coursed through my veins a full six months earlier than it should have. He didn't know I could burn it away—what would have erased the memory from any other fae under twenty-five.

I had never been more grateful for my stoic friend. His calm, collected presence quelled the rising terror in my chest. Sage would have been hysterical. I might be comforting her right now instead of the other way around. How lucky I was to have a friend who could comfort me without all the troubling emotions that weighed on land fae. Sometimes it was truly a curse.

"We will avoid him at all costs. If you are out of earshot, he cannot compel you to act." His voice was steady, but his grip on my hands tightened.

"I'm expected at court. My sister will be the princess. He could compel me to do any number of traitorous things once she's on the throne." Each word came out clipped, panicked. My breaths turned shallow.

"The prince of Summer does not have cause to attend court functions in Spring outside of weddings and war. We will avoid him until your sister is married, and then you'll likely never see him again."

I nodded, my thrashing heart slowing a fraction. I could do this. I could avoid the prince until my sister's wedding. Then, we would be safe, and I would never cross the border into Summer so long as I lived.

CHAPTER 7

Kaspar

The rain that fell in four hour intervals at midday and midnight had finally ceased. I slipped my arm from beneath Sav's head, careful not to wake her. The loss of her warmth was immediate, a hollow ache that consumed me. My gaze lingered on the pillow cradling her cheek, and I cursed it for daring to take my place.

But time was no indulgence I could afford. I had been right to mistrust Prince Fero. Now three months of meticulous maneuvering lay ahead if I meant to keep Sav from becoming a pawn in his political games. I had always known her fate would entwine with the courts once her sister wed a Hawthorn, but I had hoped for more time.

Marriage might have shielded her from some of what awaited, but my people would never accept a land fae as their princess. I was expected to wed for alliance. And since Firethorn, Mab forbade sea and land from binding themselves in such a way. If I took her as my bride, she would be forced to abandon the shore forever. My wild princess would come to despise the prison beneath the waves, and I could not condemn her to the same solitude that may one day break me.

40

SPRING

Letting the darkness devour me, I moved silently through the palace, sliding out a side door on silent feet.

Reaching the edge of Spring, I dove into my lake, tail forming as I swam for the castle nestled on the lake floor. It was centered at the bottom of the largest and deepest lake in Faerie. Once, my father had told me the magic of our line had created it. Where all the land was supposed to have been imagined by Mab, a being from unknown origins, it was a sea fae, one of my great ancestors, who brought water to Faerie.

A silly fish tale of course. The land could not have thrived without water, much as water could not be contained without land. Unlike the high fae who were bound by Mab's laws, sea fae did not consider Mab queen over our domain. We acknowledged her sovereignty on land but, though we no longer had a king or queen of our own, we were not her subjects. Still, to us, Mab was the closest thing to a deity in Faerie. Had the marriage between her son and one of ours not gone so horribly wrong, things might be quite different between us.

Stopping outside high lake stone walls, I glanced up in annoyance. A deep indigo mane of seaweed hair bobbed with the current, letting me know my night sentinel was at her post. "Mira, for Oceanus's sake," I snapped. Large navy eyes appeared over the wall and she scrambled back. In moments, the doors swung wide, and I swam through, frowning up at her as I passed.

I raced down stone halls, stopping outside my study.

Stepping through the air bubble I'd erected in the room, my tail split, forming legs and I moved to the wall of scrolls, scanning the shelves.

"Brother."

Jaw tightening, I turned to face Mira. "Yes?"

Mira stepped through the wall of air, transforming her legs and dropped, soaking wet, into my chair.

"Must you always drench everything you touch?"

"Will you invite me to the next fae ball you attend?"

I rolled my eyes. Mira was the only creature I didn't fear showing my true self to. Most of it. Though she was a horrid spy and an even worse guard, she was the one fae in Faerie I trusted implicitly. "I've told you a dozen times. It would be impossible to explain you at court."

"I could come as your lover."

I choked on a laugh. "My lover? And when we are expected to show each other affection. Would you kiss your half-brother on the lips to sell our story?"

She made a face. "Gross. Never." Leaning back in my chair, she tipped her head to the ceiling. "But we're sea folk. No one will expect us to be affectionate in public."

Although she wasn't wrong, the fiercest part of me still dreaded any-one—anyone but Sav—discovering her truth. Sav would never know it all; the knowledge was too dangerous. Yet she knew enough of Mira's magic to protect her, should the need arise.

My crown shielded me. Mira had no such defense. A half-blood born of a prince and a wild nixie, she would be hunted for sport. To most she passed for an ordinary kelpie, favoring my features. But there were so few of us left in the sea that questions would rise.

And if she ever slipped, if her magic came alive before the court, her parentage would be revealed in an instant.

"It's not safe. Land fae are vicious creatures."

Mira leaned forward. "Please, brother. I know the risks. I'll be careful. But I can't stay down here forever. Sav will lie for me. Let me go with her. No one below will know."

I spun away from my younger sister, searching the wall for the scroll I'd come down to find. "You're supposed to be guarding the gate." She huffed, and I bit back my smile. Reaching for a slender silver tube, I unlatched it, sliding out the parchment trapped inside and scrolled its contents. I turned around, facing Mira. "I'll make a bargain with you."

Mira's eyes widened and her lips split in a wide smile showing two rows of sharp teeth. "Yes. Anything."

"I will allow you to accompany me—"

"Yes. Yes!"

"Let me finish."

Mira closed her mouth, pressing a finger to her lips to silence herself.

"If you remain with Sav while you are on land and keep an eye on her." I raised a brow. "No sneaking off to explore the castle unless she's with you."

She nodded several times, lips stretching up as she fought to contain her excitement.

"Mira. I mean it. You are not permitted on land by yourself and you're never to be without me or Sav."

A squeal burst from her mouth, and she flew from her chair, barreling into me. She squeezed me with all her Nixie strength, and I gasped. "Sorry. Sorry." She loosened her hold and buried her head in my chest. "You have all my gratitude brother. All of it."

My arms came around her and for a moment, I was envious of her ability to show emotion so openly. Even if she knew the danger as much as I did, it never stopped her from being her true self with me. I longed to unwind some of my careful restraint and show a fraction of the elation she did on a given day. Her glee was contagious, but it couldn't thaw the stone lodged in my gut. A sea fae bursting with so much emotion would be discovered, eventually. One day, I would have to find a place where she would be safe.

In the same moment I wondered if it wasn't her nixie mother she got her emotion from, but our father. Was he the defective one? Was it the reason I suffered the same affliction?

"I'm going back to my post," Mira announced. She fled the room, slipping seamlessly into kelpie form as she departed.

A faint smile touched my lips, her excitement reaching even my cold heart, and I dropped into my wet chair, unrolling the scroll in my hands to read it once more.

The Prince would offer any bargain to keep this information private, I was certain. A secret like this didn't just threaten his reputation, it threatened his claim. And that made it more valuable than any army.

If I played it right, it might be enough to protect Sav.

CHAPTER 8

Sav

It had been a week since the ball. A week since Alder had formally declared his intentions for my sister, and she had begun making preparations to move into the palace in earnest. I'd missed it, too drunk on henbane wine and the poison-tipped flora of the hedge maze. A fact Sage hadn't stopped reminding me of. I couldn't tell her the truth. That a prince from another court knew my name.

With the formal engagement looming, I needed leverage—or a believable excuse. But short of dying, my family wouldn't let me skip it. So, option one it was.

Fero wasn't my only concern though. Magic pressed against my skin, making me feverish, begging for release. It was becoming increasingly difficult to hide it from my family. While I longed to share it with Sage, she was terrible at keeping secrets, and if Uncle found out, he would sell me to whichever noble offered him the best price. The idea of someone choosing me for my gift alone made me sick.

A knock sounded at my door. "Enter."

I looked up from the vanity in my temporary palace room. Uncle believed it was to our advantage to spend as much time as possible here so the nobles began to think of us as members of the court. That meant arriving a full day before the other guests.

I managed a smile as Primrose stepped in, her presence a welcome distraction.

"I'm so happy to see you," she said, crossing the room and taking my hands.

"I've never been gladder to see a friendly face," I breathed. An attendant had laced me tighter than Sage ever had, and my vision darkened at the corners as I stood. I swayed on my feet.

"Whoa there, let me help you." Primrose unclasped our hands, moving behind me and began tugging at my laces.

"That's much better," I exhaled.

Primrose moved in a circle, eyeing me. "Gorgeous gown, but don't you think something dark would suit your complexion?"

I glanced down, smoothing my rose-gold gown. "I prefer green, but at court, we're expected to dress in the pastel colors of Spring, are we not?"

Primrose laughed, twirling to emphasize her bright fuchsia fabric. "As long as we aren't caught in shades of white, bronze or blue, I say what's the harm?"

"What about Autumn? Would it not be wrong to wear their colors?"

Primrose fluttered her lashes demurely. "Autumn has an unwed prince who I've heard is on the market for a bride. If I were a bolder lady, I might select something red."

"Why, Primrose Magnolia," I said, aiming for playfulness, "do you have plans to catch a prince?"

Her easy smile faltered for a moment, and butterflies erupted in my stomach. Court life was a mystery to me, and she was my first potential friend here. I didn't want to ruin it.

She recovered quickly, pink lips forming a pout. "We can't all have princes falling at our feet. Some of us are forced to find creative means for catching a male's eye."

I pasted a smile onto my face, swallowing my nerves.

Someone knocked on my door, and Primrose glanced toward it. "Could that be one of your royal suitors now?"

I wiped slick palms on my skirts before moving to answer.

Sage burst into the room, and I jumped backward, narrowly missing the door as it swung wide. "It's horrible. I have nothing to say to him." She halted, eyes going wide as her gaze landed on Primrose. "Pardon me," she stuttered. "I wasn't aware Sav had a guest." The accusation in her tone was clear. Sage hated when I had anything of my own. My *guest* would now be her sole focus for the night. If the evening didn't end with Primrose being her new best friend, I would never hear the end of it.

Primrose dipped her chin, and Sage's elation at her show of deference wafted through the room. "Lady Primrose. A pleasure."

Sage's brows flattened. "Cousin to my betrothed?"

Primrose nodded. "The one and only."

"How do you know my sister?"

Could she have made her envy any less plain?

"I met Sav on the night of your betrothal." Her gaze slid to me, and she smiled. "She and I commiserated over the overwhelming amount of testosterone at the party."

I winced as Sage's hot stare burned the side of my face. Her tongue-lashing would come later. In private. Speaking that way with a stranger—a member of the royal family no less—was the worst possible betrayal the Briar family could imagine. It spoke of our low birth and even lower standing.

For a moment we all stared at one another, Sage unwilling to go, Primrose too polite to ask, and I terrified I might have drunkenly spilled any one of our family secrets.

"Well, I should be going," Primrose said, breaking the silence. "Sav, sit with me at dinner?"

I cleared my throat.

"She'll be needed by my side, I'm afraid." Sage grinned, but it was all teeth.

SPRING

I winced. I could think of a dozen places I'd rather sit tonight, but my sister's nerves were live wires sparking in agitation. So much tension in the air made my stomach churn, and I clenched my hands into fists. If it were me in Sage's place, I would want her by my side. I swallowed, nodding to Primrose, and she turned, leaving us.

At least it was a private dinner. Alder's and his bride's family members only. The one bright spot in what promised to be a dreadful evening. And one more night to figure out how to outmaneuver Prince Fero before he made his next move.

CHAPTER 9

Kaspar

A week had been more than enough time to send my spies into Summer to gather what intel I could on Prince Fero. But his wide open palace, visible from the sea, made it harder than I'd anticipated to search his court. My spies were forbidden from setting one fin in the ocean and if any had been caught it would have meant their death. Worse, my uncle, Prince Aegon of Oceans and Seas, may have taken it as an act of war, and my army was no match for his.

With several centuries on me, his magic was at its zenith, where mine was only just beginning to gain strength. When my parents had been murdered nearly two decades ago, poisoned by an unknown court's assassin, Prince Aegon, who had been as close with my father as two sea fae could be, had severed ties without a word and staged his army at each of the access points to his domain, declaring the sea off limits to me and leaving me bereft of any blood relatives apart from Mira.

Neither I nor my parents had expected me to begin learning what it meant to rule for centuries. They'd left a gaping wound with their absence and an even greater weight on my shoulders. At eleven, the burden and heartache of their loss and all my new responsibilities consumed me, leaving little room to ponder the bigger picture. I hadn't considered whether Summer was in league with him, but of the two courts bordered by oceans and seas, only Summer's castle was near his court's shore.

Were Princes Aegon and Fero colluding against me?

Summer was short on many resources. Where they were rich in gold, salt, and the deadly plants used to create weapons in battle, they lacked fresh water and many of the healing herbs only found in Spring.

Spring suffered no shortage of resources. In many ways, it was the richest court. Their mines produced the only source of resin, desired by all, and the herbs required for most healing tonics originated in their forests. They relied heavily on the earth magic their princess brought to keep them thriving. It was one of the many reasons that, though a great deal of their land was eaten up by my principality, they were afforded the same respect as all the other courts.

"I'm ready!" Mira appeared in my office, waterproof bag in hand.

"We're not going to dinner," I reminded her.

She pouted, lower lip jutting out. "You said I could if Sav would be there."

I stood, pushing back my chair, my spine popping as I stretched. After hours pouring over reports, I could use a break, even if it was to verbally spar with my sister. "Tonight is for the family, but I agree you should see more of Spring before we formally go to court. What do you say to a bit of spying?"

Mira dropped her bag on my desk. "Hell yes."

I bit back my grin. "Come on, then."

Tracing the path upstream to Spring Castle's closest border, we stopped in the stream bisecting the Maywood, listening for the sound of patrols. I held a finger to my lips as leaves crackled on land. I rose, eyes just above the water, and scanned the forest for the source of the noise. Crunching footsteps to my left had my gaze shooting toward it.

In moments, a fox appeared, hopping a fallen log, and I froze. He wasn't just any woodland creature. His eyes were fae bright, telling me he was a shifter, like me. He ran past, never glancing my way. When minutes stretched and I was sure he wouldn't double back, I motioned for Mira to rise, and together we left the water.

We shifted into land fae form, and I dried myself, conjuring velvet slacks. Mira pulled a dress out of her bag and tugged it over her wet form. As only half sea-fae, some of my gifts eluded her, and drying herself magically was one of them. Mira's wide grin spoke of how little she cared that she was dripping if it meant another chance to be on land.

I motioned for her to follow as we moved silently through the forest, stopping along the tree line outside Spring's gardens. I had spent more nights than I cared to count in these woods, but most led me to a small home at the edge of a clearing, far from court and the nobles whose sprawling estates surrounded it.

When the orcs circling the gardens passed, I darted forward, into the boxwood maze, and Mira dashed after me. Thus far, she'd remained true to her word—silent. I flicked my wrist, shoving the bushes apart, and we moved through them, carefully avoiding the golden jays' watchful eyes. Though they were beautiful, they were also the eyes and ears of General Creig. He had proved a worthy adversary, and nothing gave me greater pleasure than slipping past him.

"We'll need to run for it from here. Can you keep up?" I pitched my voice low so no passersby would hear. Mira nodded, that wide grin still plastered on her face, and I turned, tracking two orcs disappearing around a corner. "Now," I breathed and raced across the lawn. I reached the wall, pressing my back against it, and Mira stopped beside me. Pride swelled in my chest. She was getting better. If only I could tell my court what she was—who she was—so she would claim her place by my side.

Inching around the stone facade, we halted by a set of massive windows and ducked below the bushes rimming them. Crouched against the wall, I looked Mira over for any bit of jewelry or bobble that might glint in the light and catch someone's attention. She'd come prepared, though, and melted seamlessly into the shadows. "We'll go in turns. I'll keep a lookout while you spy, then you'll do the same for me. Understand?"

She nodded.

"If I tap your leg, drop below the bushes immediately. No questions."

I let Mira go first, and she rose, pressing an ear to glass. With the bright fae lights twinkling inside, the world beyond the window would be black, and it gave us the perfect opportunity to gather intel. There was nothing useful to overhear, but Mira would learn names and faces. That alone would serve her well at the ball tomorrow.

I watched the dark garden, alert for any sign of Creig's soldiers, and let my mind wander. I needed a new strategy for tomorrow's ball. I would need to put some distance between myself and Sav. If she was Fero's target because of me, better to let him believe she wasn't important to me. In truth, it was better to distance myself from her in the eyes of all at court.

Mira dropped beside me. "They're all so glamorous," she said. "And the prince is handsome. Sage must be overjoyed to be marrying him."

"Do not speak with the prince tomorrow night. That is nonnegotiable."

"That wasn't a condition of your bargain."

My jaw tightened. *Tricked by my own sister. Embarrassing.* Still, Sav wouldn't go near Prince Alder for anything, and that meant Mira couldn't either. "True, but you must stay with Sav or me. Remember that."

A cunning glint entered Mira's eyes, and I wondered what scheme she was concocting. Whatever it was, neither Sav nor I would fall victim to it. I was content with that fact.

I rose, peering inside through the glass, and my heart stuttered in my chest. Sav was seated by her sister as I'd expected. Alder sat at the head of the table, his cousin, the female I'd met before, beside him. None of that gave me pause. Sav leaned toward the male to her left, and my blood ran cold. Prince Fero laid his hand over hers and whispered something in her ear.

She smiled—fucking smiled—and my world zeroed in on his finger, tracing a circle on the back of her hand. I had to get in there, to save her, but Mira was with me, and I wouldn't risk her, even for Sav. Damn my ignorance. I had spies watching him day and night, and no one had reported this. Why was he there? This dinner was for family only.

Mira poked my leg, and I snapped out of my trance, dropping beside her. "What is it? What did you see?"

"Nothing. It's my turn."

Ice chilled my veins. "We're leaving. *Now*."

I grabbed Mira's wrist, damning spy protocol, and dragged her across the lawn. She dug her heels into the grass, fighting my grip, but she was no match for me, and I pulled her into the bushes.

"Kaspar. Stop it!" She thrashed in my iron hold, nails attempting to pry my fingers from her wrist, but I was impervious to any of it. Red tinged the edge of my vision as I continued through the bushes and back to the stream.

"Get in."

"No. You promised!" She punched my arm, and I spun to face her.

"Get in the water and go home. If you don't, there will be no ball tomorrow."

"You can't. We made a bargain."

I ground my teeth, feeling a few sharp spikes snap off. "I never said which ball. If I take you to a ball the next time the prince marries, I'll be fulfilling my end of the bargain. Get in the water or kiss your night of merriment goodbye."

Mira's hands balled at her sides, jaw set, but when I turned, she flinched. Her fury fizzled under the weight of mine. Expression smoothing, she nodded once and turned, diving into the stream. I watched her go, waiting a moment to ensure she wouldn't double back.

SPRING

Taking several calming breaths, I ran a hand through my hair and schooled my features into neutrality, striding for the main doors of Spring's palace.

CHAPTER 10

Sav

"What if we all play a game in the gardens?" Sage glanced hopefully between me and her prince.

"I don—"

"Excellent idea," Prince Fero said, cutting me off. "Don't you think, Lady?"

I swallowed my protest, lips forming a smile. What was I doing? When the prince shocked us all by appearing at dinner, I had thought it best to pretend to befriend him. In public, with others watching, he wouldn't force me to do anything, but the gardens were full of dark corners and the memory of my palm pressed to poison-tipped blooms was sharp in my mind.

He made me do that. But he didn't expect me to remember. If he learned the truth—that my magic had burned away his compulsion six months before it should have—there was no telling what he'd do with yet another of my secrets. I had to keep pretending.

The prince traced a lazy circle over the back of my hand, and I stilled my trembling fingers. Primrose eyed us, and ice ran up my spine. What had I told her in the maze?

The doors to the dining room swung open, and Kaspar strode in. His gait was more brusque than usual and he wore a shirt and coat for once. My shoulders relaxed, and I exhaled a steady breath. I tracked his movement as he stopped beside Alder and dipped his chin. "I heard you were having a party and forgot to invite me."

Prince Alder's wild gaze darted around the table—looking for his brother, no doubt—and a bead of sweat dotted his brow. "Your invitation must have been delayed. I would never dream of excluding our oldest ally." His eyes flicked to Prince Fero, and my stomach flipped.

Was I a pawn in some game between princes? I blew out a breath, shaking the thought away. Whatever they were up to, it could only be some play for power. If anyone here was at risk of being used, it was my sister.

Without waiting for that invitation, Kaspar stalked to an empty seat on the other side of the table, beside Primrose, and my heart sank. What was he doing over there? So far away? All the hope swelling inside me died when he slid into the seat and lifted her hand to his lips. Whatever had brought him here tonight, it wasn't me. The prince had come on business.

"Shall we?" Sage asked, snapping my focus away from Kaspar. Her eyes met each of ours expectantly. "The gardens?"

The silence hung between us, no one saying anything.

Prince Fero stood. "Lead the way, Lady."

Sage's cheeks flushed, and she dipped her chin, glancing at her fiancé. "My prince?"

Alder tugged at his collar, grimacing as though he'd swallowed a lemon, but he rose from his chair. "Let us change into more appropriate attire and meet in the gardens." He swept from the room, not sparing any of us a backward glance. The reminder to my sister that royals didn't attend a new function without a change of wardrobe was a jab no one missed, and pink stained Sage's cheeks.

I jumped from my seat, skirting around Prince Fero, careful to avoid eye contact. His gaze burned over me, and I felt sharp eyes narrow in on the pulse jumping at my throat. "I'll see you out there," I said to the room, biting my lip and hoping he hadn't heard the quiver in my voice.

"I'll come with you." Primrose stood, extracting her hand from Kaspar's and glided around the table, hooking her arm through mine.

"Wait for me," Sage said, pushing back her chair and joining us as we departed.

In the hall, away from all that power, I inhaled sharply, holding a hand to my tightly constrained chest. Outside; in the dark—where everything might be deadly, including the prince—I would have no defense. Except my magic, which I couldn't use. Inhale. Exhale. Inhale.

"Sav, do you want to borrow one of my dresses?" Primrose stared at me as I struggled to compose my erratic thoughts.

"Yes, please."

"Do you have another?" Sage asked in a light voice. Her nails dug into my arm, and though I would have scolded her normally, the pain shook me from my daze.

"Sure." Primrose glanced my way as I worked to push the terror down. *Act normal.* I couldn't let them know what was happening. What might happen.

We pushed through Primrose's door, and even in my anxious state, my mouth fell open as I took in its splendor. It was five times the size of my room; black walls papered in a delicate fleur-de-lis pattern. Glass vases sat atop stone pillars, filled to the brim with gardenias and soft pink roses, their floral scent floating on some invisible breeze. The juxtaposition of black against pastel pink stole my breath. It was so different from the rest of the castle. The palace was a study in browns and greens with bright pops of color throughout, alive with vines and flora.

This room was something out of a dream. Nothing living crawled along its walls; even the flowers decorating it were decapitated blooms, already dying. In Spring, it bordered on treason. My gaze traveled the expansive space, stopping on Primrose.

Our eyes met.

"It's... lovely."

A vein twitching under her eye stilled, and her lips twisted up. "I decorated it myself."

There was something in her words, this exchange, that I was missing, but my jumbled thoughts could only focus on one mystery at a time. I would puzzle it out later.

Sage flopped onto the bed, staring up at a solid black ceiling, covered in tiny twinkling fae lights. A mimicry of the night sky. "He hardly looks at me." She sighed and lifted her head, gaze shooting to me. "Don't you think it's odd? We're to be married, and he hardly looks at me."

Primrose poked her head out of her closet. "He's a male. Males only look when you're naked."

I smothered a laugh, grateful for their silly girl talk. It took my mind off what was coming.

"He looks at other females." Sage crossed her arms, her gaze flicking to me, and bile rose in my throat. The barb had found its mark.

Primrose reappeared with her hands full of gowns, and I moved to help her with them. Together, we laid out fabric across her bed. Sage kicked her foot, knocking a dress off the bed. Primrose lowered her brows at my sister, but she didn't notice. I wanted to make excuses for her, but I was in no mood to defend Sage tonight. I had problems of my own.

"Here, Sav. This one will bring a glow to your tanned skin."

I held out my hand, taking a deep emerald gown from her, and bit my lip. It was the most beautiful gown I had ever seen. "I don't know," I said.

Primrose held a deep charcoal gown up, inspecting herself in the mirror. Like her cousins, her hair was more sandy brown than red, and the deep color of the fabric made her eyes sparkle. She grinned at me. "Well, I do." Her gaze flicked to my sister. "Get up, Sage. Your fiancé is waiting, and Alder doesn't like to wait."

Sage sat up, looking truly concerned. "What are you both wearing? Those drab gowns are hideous."

"It's a night game in the gardens. The point is to hide. Do you want them to find you?"

Sage narrowed her eyes at Primrose. "Why wouldn't I?"

Arms linked, we strode down the long corridor, nervous energy crackling in the surrounding air. I wasn't sure of Primrose's motives, but I liked her, and something in my gut told me to trust her. Still, when we passed the hall of blooms, I hunched my shoulders, thankful to be in the middle. It didn't stop them from stretching toward us, but they didn't die the way they had upon arrival, and Primrose watched Sage instead of me. *Good*.

Stepping into the dark, my heart stuttered, and I swallowed hard. "Sage. Don't leave me. Please."

Sage released my arm. "Sav, stop whining. Go hide. And let Prince Fero find you." Without a backward glance, she vanished into the darkness. Hollowness carved through my chest. Had Sage been the one to invite him tonight? At our uncle's bidding?

Primrose tugged me close, her breath brushing my ear. "Come on. I won't give them the advantage. Let's hide."

I glanced back at the slip of pale pink peeking from beneath a hedge. My sister wouldn't do this to me. Would she? The memory of her fury when Alder had found me burned hot beneath my ribs. No. She couldn't be that cruel. She was my sister. My twin. We were supposed to look out for each other.

"They'll see her," I whispered.

"She wants to be found."

I didn't argue. Sage wasn't doing anything to blend in. She stood directly in the moon's path. Of course, she wanted to be found. Her prince would meet her at the altar. The one stalking me had nefarious motives I couldn't fathom.

We slipped into the hedge maze, the golden jays flitting ahead to light our path. Primrose squeezed my arm, urging silence. A rustle stirred the leaves at our side, and I swallowed a scream. She pressed a finger to her lips and glided forward on soundless feet.

I was lost in the twisting green, but Primrose knew the way. She had grown up within these walls—cousin to two princes, the only daughter of her line. No parents. No guidance. Just like Alder and Foxglove. The three of them had carved out their childhood in this castle long before Sage and I were born, long before their parents were claimed by Autumn's war.

Were her cousins kind? I didn't think so. From what little I knew of them, Alder was insufferable. Foxglove was a mystery, but I didn't trust him. I didn't trust any Hawthorn. It was a good thing Primrose was a Magnolia.

A clicking noise sounded to our left, and I jumped, goosebumps erupting on my arms. Primrose tugged us farther into the maze. She pulled more insistently, and I began to question her intentions. "Where are we going?" I whispered.

She didn't answer, pulling me along, and ice raced up my spine. I dug my heels into the grass, yanking my arm free. She spun around, searching my face. "Come on," she mouthed.

I shook my head. "Where are we going?"

She pointed deeper into the maze, but I crossed my arms over my chest. She threw up her arms in exasperation. "Away from Prince Fero," she whispered, and I froze.

A jolt of fear surged through me. What did she know? I had met Primrose the same night I met Prince Fero. Was that a coincidence? I wouldn't stay to find out.

I turned around, putting distance between us, zigzagging back the way I'd come. Branches scraped against my bare arms, snagging on fabric and catching my hair. I swallowed a scream as something snapped behind me and ran faster.

Leaves crunched, and magic swelled in the air. My heart beat against my ribcage, my corset the only thing keeping it from exploding from my chest. What did she want? What did *they* want with me?

I burst free of the maze.

Arms wrapped around me, lifting me off the ground, and lips pressed against my ear. "You're mine."

My heart stuttered. Not again. Not him. Please, not—

"No!" I screamed, wedging my elbow into a solid chest. He grunted, but didn't release me, and I wrapped my fingers around cool, scaled arms, digging my nails in. *Cool. scaled.* My heart slowed, my head jerked to the left, and aquamarine hair tickled my nose.

"Kaspar," I gasped, inhaling my first real breath since Prince Fero had arrived that evening. He set me down, and I spun to face him, throwing my arms around him. "I'm so glad you're here." I squeezed him tightly, wetness pooling in my lashes as I shut my eyes and inhaled his scent.

"I'm here," he said against my ear.

He released me and I exhaled a slow breath, wiping my eyes. "I want to go."

He searched my face, nodding, and spun around, pulling me behind him. We stepped through an arched doorway, into the palace, and the trembling in my hands stilled. We moved silently, stopping outside the door to my temporary room. His fingers flexed in mine, and he faced me. "Let's go to my castle. I can protect you there."

I blinked. "I... can't... My sister. The wedding. I have to be here. I—"

There was a moment of silence, and though his face was a mask, I knew Kaspar considered every angle before he spoke.

"You're right. Come on." He pushed the door open and stepped inside. I followed numbly, some of my fear ebbing away. Here, with Kaspar, I would be safe.

CHAPTER 11

Kaspar

I pressed my lips to Sav's temple. She twitched in her sleep, rolling onto her side, and I slid down beside her, an arm draped across her waist. When I'd found her, terror had bound her like a noose, and something inside me had snapped. Her relief, when she realized it was me who held her, was the only thing that stitched me together again.

I was a fool. All my careful plans unraveled the moment fear for her seized me. What had I become—this creature who acted without thought, who bared his hand so recklessly? Sav would be my death, but I didn't seem to care.

The plan had been simple. Sit with the spring court emissary. Charm her. Convince them all that Sav meant nothing more to me than any other female. But even as I smiled at Primrose, my gaze betrayed me, drawn back, again and again, to Sav. To Prince Fero's hand idly tracing circles along her skin. The sight made my blood burn. I longed to cross the table, snap off the offending hand, and feed it to my eels.

The soft patter of an animal's footfall sounded in the hall, and I sat up. It drew near, and I stood, slipping into a dark corner. The door creaked open, and I prepared to pounce.

I was frozen as a shining black nose sniffed the air and bright amethyst eyes darted to me. For a moment we stared at one another. A dozen thoughts raced through my mind. End the spring court spy. Destroy it before it could use this information to bring me down. Learn who it was and bribe the shifter. It backed up, and before I had made up my mind, it disappeared.

I darted into the hall, looking left, then right, but it was gone.

What did that mean for me? Why had it come to Sav's room? Who did it report to?

And then there was Primrose. She had the unsettling habit of appearing where she wasn't expected and vanishing without anyone remembering she was there to begin with.

There were too many questions; not enough answers. Sav wouldn't be safe here, but no one else would enter her room tonight. Not with my scent lingering. Leaving Sav's room, I moved through the shadows, drawing the darkness to me, and when I reached the stream, I dove in.

I slammed my office door and leaned against it. Was I battling my uncle, Summer, Spring? They were all suspects, and one thing was clear: Sav would be the pawn who suffered. I had to protect her. It began with ensuring no one knew how powerful she would become. She had six months until she completed the ceremony to reveal her magic. Fire magic wouldn't wait patiently, though. When it came, it would demand a price.

It was less than three months until Sage's wedding, until the twins moved into the palace permanently. I was sure nothing I said would convince Sav not to go. She was loyal to her wretched sister despite all Sage did to her. The most dangerous time would be the months following the wedding. When she lived in the castle, but shouldn't have magic yet.

SPRING

In my room, I swam through a seaweed curtain and moved to the bed of sea holly at the center of my room, anchoring myself. I needed sleep. Needed to be refreshed to face my foes come morning, but even with exhaustion weighing my lids down, my mind raced, replaying the evening's events and all I'd learned on a loop.

The more my mind turned over each moment, the more it came back to one fae. Her covert glances at Sav, the way she watched the summer prince nearly as closely as I did. How she seemed to disappear without anyone noticing.

Primrose.

Soft light filtered through crystal waters, and even at this depth I knew I had overslept. Untangling myself from my bed, I started when a pair of deep indigo eyes fixed on mine.

"Oceanus! Mira, you startled me."

In kelpie form, she never quite resembled the rest of us. Something otherworldly clung to her, a wildness that betrayed her nixie blood. She blinked, baring two rows of sharp teeth, and I stiffened.

"It's early for a challenge, isn't it?"

"You treated me like one of your subjects last night," she hissed.

I blinked away the remnants of sleep. "You *are* my subject."

Bubbles burst from her nostrils as she snorted, then lunged. I shifted, teeth flashing as I snapped at her snout. She reared back, hooves striking the sea-glass floor, shards scattering as she charged again.

I lashed her cheek with my tail. She froze, stunned, as a bloom of indigo blood drifted between us.

Eyes wide, she spun and bolted from the chamber.

My heart thudded painfully in my chest. "Mira! Wait!"

But she didn't. And though guilt pricked at me, I did not follow. Life would be far crueler to her if she never learned her place. I loathed reminding her she was not royal—loathed being not only her brother, but her prince. Yet had she spoken to another of my court as she had to me, I could not have shielded her from the retribution that followed.

Sighing, I galloped down the hall to my study. Judging by the light overhead, I had only a few hours before the evening's ball. There were two fae in all of Faerie who might help me. One in Winter and one in Spring. My gut said asking for aid outside Spring was dangerous, but there was a plot unfolding there whose players were unclear to me, and that made asking anyone in Sav's court a risk as well.

I pressed through the air bubble, shifting, and crossed the room to my stack of books, pulling out the one labeled: *The Wildwood - Maps of Spring Forests and Territories*. Setting it down atop my desk, I flipped pages until I found the March Forest. It was three days from the spring castle by hoof, but there were a few streams that would bring me there in half the time.

Tracing the path with my finger, I stabbed a small stream running along Spring and Autumn's border. It was the quickest path, and from there, the trek to the satyrs' stronghold would only be another day.

"Brother."

I slammed the book shut, looking up. Mira hovered inside the door in fae form, a waterproof bag clutched tightly in her fist. A thin blue line bisected her cheek, and I winced. The cut had to be deep if it was still healing. She straightened, moving to my chair and sitting rigidly.

I folded my arms across my chest. "I'm working, Mira."

"I won't let you slip out without me. We made a bargain."

"I'm not attending tonight's ball. You'll go to the next one."

Mira's eyes narrowed, nostrils flaring, and she wrapped her fingers around the armrest of my chair. "A bargain is a bargain."

I sighed. I truly didn't have time for her antics tonight. The sooner I reached the March Forest, the sooner I could breathe easy. "I have other matters to attend to tonight."

"I'll stay with Sav. You agreed I could be with her *or* you."

I raised an eyebrow, but my shoulders relaxed. Mira at the spring court while I was not could benefit us both. Surely my enemies wouldn't attack Sav with a kelpie by her side. It would give me extra time as well.

"You're right. We made a bargain."

Mira exhaled, grip loosening.

"But."

She tensed again, nails digging into the seaweed armrests.

"You will go as Emissary of Lakes and Streams, and you will not leave Sav's side until I return for you."

A grin split Mira's turquoise lips, and she jumped up from her chair, flinging her arms around me. "Oh brother. Please stay away for days and days. Sav and I will be on our best behavior."

My lips twitched, and reluctantly, I wrapped my arms around her. "I *am* sorry the lake is not a kinder place to you, Mir."

It was a reminder of why they needed my protection. Mira and Sav, unwanted in places they should've ruled, their power seen as threat instead of promise.

CHAPTER 12

Sav

My fork scraped too loudly against porcelain as Primrose slipped into the seat beside me. I glanced at her from beneath my lashes. She lifted a spoon, dipped it into her custard, and kept her gaze fixed ahead.

The silence thickened. I shifted in my chair, grip tightening around the fork.

In the light of midday, I questioned my hysteria the night before. She had done nothing to warrant my suspicion, and I hadn't truly known where she was taking me.

"Would you pass the sea salt?"

I blinked and nodded, reaching across the long stone table and sliding a bowl of pink salt with a delicate bronze spoon in it toward her.

"You have my gratitude."

I frowned, gaze returning to my plate, and lifted my fork to my lips.

"Sav, are we to be enemies? I cannot fathom what I've done to earn your mistrust."

My stomach sank, and I met her gaze. Periwinkle eyes sparkled in the sunlight as she searched my face. The true concern in her eyes had me swallowing down all the silly thoughts I'd had the night before. Primrose had been nothing but kind since I'd arrived at court. Soon, we would live here together. What reason could she have for plotting against me?

I set my fork down, swallowed a carrot, and turned to face her. "No. Of course not. Last night was—"

"My fault." She cut me off. "Please forgive me. I should have been honest with you." My throat went dry as I waited for her to continue, imagining three different ways this conversation might go. "I have long valued female friendship over a male. To let all that go out the window over a crush. I'm ashamed of myself."

I blinked, struggling to make sense of her words. Crush? "What?"

Color rose in her cheeks as she looked away. "Your friend. Prince Kaspar."

"What?!"

"If you care for him, tell me. I would never dream of coming between you."

I caught her hands in mine. "No. Primrose, there's no romantic affection between us." The ache in my chest was only the urgency to make her believe me.

A tentative smile curved her lips. "Truly? I was certain there was something. Jealousy was eating me alive."

I squeezed her fingers. My dearest friend deserved someone who would cherish him—and selfishly, I adored the thought of him spending more time at court. "I swear it. Nothing could be further from the truth."

A laugh escaped me, and her grin widened, lighting her whole face.

A throat cleared, and we looked at the doorway. "Ladies."

"Kaspar!" I stood, pushing my chair back when Mira stepped through the door behind him. "Mira!"

She pushed past her older brother, raced into the room and tackled me with one of her violent hugs. I slid back, bumping the table.

"Emissary, comport yourself in court."

I stifled a laugh at Kaspar's rigid words, but Mira released me, jumping back as though I'd stung her. "Apologies, Lady Briar. I have come to court to represent Lakes and Streams while our honorable prince attends to other matters."

I struggled to flatten my lips into a serious expression. Mira adored being on land. Coming to court as the emissary of her principality was brilliant and some plot of Kaspar's no doubt. I grinned at him, but his face was a mask of cold indifference.

A shudder rolled through me. I so rarely saw the princely face he showed the world, and it chilled my veins. But with only us and Primrose in the room, I didn't know who he was acting the part for.

Land and water fae could never truly be matched. Mab wouldn't allow it. I hadn't said as much to Primrose, but she surely knew the rules better than I. She might get him into bed, but never past the door to the throne room. Not while Mab ruled.

Primrose stood. "A pleasure to meet you, Emissary. As emissary to Spring, we must become close acquaintances."

Mira grinned from ear to ear and lifted Primrose's fingers to her lips. I stifled a laugh. Clearly, her brother had not explained the differences between male and female greetings. Primrose accepted her kiss graciously, dipping her chin to Mira.

"I'm afraid Mira is expected to remain with Sav for the duration of her stay. She will room with her and will benefit greatly from her tutelage in land fae customs."

On second thought, it was a good thing only Primrose was in the room. No one would have mistaken his tone for anything other than brotherly affection.

Mira's cheeks bloomed dark blue, and she straightened her shoulders, turning to me. "I look forward to all you have to teach me, Lady Briar."

When Kaspar left, not saying where he was going or why, Mira and I retreated to my room to prepare for the evening.

"Can you believe I get to stay here until he returns?" Mira sat at the edge of my bed, gazing around the room I'd begun spending more time in than my own room back at our cottage.

"Where's he going?"

Mira glanced at me as I sat at the vanity, running a comb through my hair.

"Who cares? He said he'd be gone three or four days. That means we have half a week without him breathing down our necks!"

I smiled, watching her in the vanity mirror. Mira was beautiful in the same dangerous sort of way as her brother. Her dark strands of hair were always a little wild, but didn't float on an imaginary breeze the way Kaspar's did. Her ink-blue eyes matched her hair, but her skin held none of the scales his did. Truly, I didn't see much resemblance in them apart from the shape of their eyes and their strong noses.

In kelpie form, they were even less alike. Kaspar was enormous, his sparkling turquoise hide glorious in the sunlight. Mira's coat was so dark it was nearly black, and she seemed to swallow the light rather than draw it, but her personality couldn't be more opposite. She was sunshine itself as long as her temper remained at bay. A temper that set her apart from her brother and all the other sea folk.

It was the reason he feared for her safety. One of her parents must have been land folk, and that was dangerous. Mab strictly forbade any offspring between our two kinds. For good reason. Mira's wild, unstable magic was exactly the sort of thing Mab protected us from. One kelpie female, watched closely by her brother, could be contained. A world filled with her kind might destroy us.

"Do you think anyone will ask me to dance tonight?"

I smiled at Mira and the excitement in her voice. "Of course! A beauty like you will have the males lining up."

She grinned, sliding off the bed. "I brought a dress." She held up a tiny bag, and I frowned. Whatever dress she had brought would likely need quite a bit of pressing. Before I could object, she reached inside, pulling out a glittering bit of fabric in bright turquoise. She held it against her long frame. "What do you think? I've been waiting ages to wear it."

It was beautiful, thin and a bit revealing for our court, but as emissary to Lakes and Streams, she would be expected to uphold the traditions of her court, not ours.

"It's beautiful."

She let out a squeal, spinning in a circle.

I stood, crossed the room and ran a hand down the fabric. This close, I saw the sparkles were bits of glass refracting the sunlight. Under the twinkling fae light at tonight's ball, she would dazzle. Unfortunately, they were also sharp, and I lifted a finger to my lip, sucking the blood welling at the tip. "I hope it feels better on the inside."

Mira laughed, flipping the material over to expose smooth silk. I touched the pad of my healed finger to the fabric, wishing Spring Court fashion allowed something so exquisite. While Mira reveled in soft silk against her skin, any male thinking to wrap his hands around her would get a sharp reminder to respect her space.

When we were dressed, Mira's hair bound and tied with rows of seashell strands, we stepped through the doors to the grand ballroom and Mira tipped her head back, gasping. "It's wondrous," she breathed.

"Come on." I tugged her forward, feeling small next to the towering beauty at my side. Eyes glanced our way, landing on her with interest, and I hugged her closer to me, carefully avoiding the sharp bits of her dress. I was fiercely protective, as though she were my little sister too, and I feared what this court of snakes might try to exploit from her.

"There you are, Sav."

I stiffened as my uncle emerged before us, tawny brows arched, and tightened my grip on Mira's arm. "Who have you brought as your companion?" His hazel gaze swept over her not lingering on bare skin, but piercing deeper. Not lust. Ambition.

I drew myself to my full height, forcing my chin high though his shadow still loomed over me. "This is Mira, emissary to the court of Lakes and Streams. Emissary, may I present my uncle... Robin Goodfellow."

He inclined his head with the smoothness of a predator, lips curling in a smile that belonged to a collector who had just spotted a rare jewel. I barely resisted the urge to claw his eyes out.

As we'd practiced, Mira dipped her chin, only slightly, and I beamed with pride. Her nod was perfectly calculated—just shallow enough to remind him she outranked him.

His eyes glinted, and I recognized a plot forming in them. Before he could say more, I steered us past him, angling for the room's corner where refreshments and light bites were served. She glanced back over her shoulder, but I ignored my uncle, sliding between guests—some of whom openly stared—to the low table laden with savory sweets and drinks.

Mira reached for a glass but turned back, a question on her face.

"I'm not your keeper." My lips tipped up. "And we're at a party." I grabbed the glass beside hers, lifting it to my mouth.

Mira did the same, taking a large swig. I laughed, taking small sips of the henbane wine. Perhaps one of us should keep our wits tonight.

CHAPTER 13

Kaspar

It was dawn when I stepped out of the stream along Autumn and Spring's border. Crisp Autumn air encroached on the humidity in Spring. I magicked a coat over my shoulders, wrapping it tightly around me, and moved on light feet away from Autumn.

Harpies burst from the trees, flapping leathery wings, and I lightened my step. I didn't want to give myself away and allow the satyrs to ensnare me. While we weren't enemies exactly, they were a solitary bunch and as likely to stay hidden from me as they were to string me up for trespassing on their land.

As I trekked through the woods, my mind wandered back to the moment we'd arrived in the dining room. I'd stepped through the door, prepared to announce our presence when Primrose spoke.

"If you care for him, tell me. I would never dream of coming between you."

Sav grabbed the fae's hands, squeezing them. "No. Primrose, there's no romantic affection between us."

My stomach had dropped hearing those words, my cold heart stuttering in my chest. But of course she would believe that to be our truth. My kind didn't feel romantic affection. To admit such a thing would mean my death. I could never give her any indication of my defect. What would Faerie make of a sea prince who felt such emotion?

Why then did it hurt so much to hear her confirm the words that would keep me safe?

Her sincere expression as she reassured Primrose twisted like a knife. I rubbed absently at my chest, as if I could press the ache back into place.

This was a good thing. A necessary thing. I could never hope to convince my court—Faerie—I was the cold prince with Sav by my side. The torture of pretending every time she was near was an agony of my own making.

I stumbled, caught my footing, and shook my head. She was twisting me in knots. Making it impossible to tell which way was up and whom to trust. In the cutthroat world of Faerie, a distraction so great could mean our deaths. I had to give her up. For both our sakes. The ache in my chest pulsed like a second heartbeat. I kept walking. Motion, at least, was something I could control.

"Oh woe. Ohhhh woe is the weary traveler." A chorus of tiny voices stopped me in my tracks. Before me, a meadow opened up to a great field of buttercups. They turned their tiny heads toward me, chattering with delight. "Rest with us a while, Prince of Lore. Your head is heavy, your heart sore." Several golden cups nodded in agreement.

I stroked the petals of the nearest buttercup, holding out a hand. She climbed into my palm, giving me a dazzling smile. "I would not give you my burden, fair maidens."

Another chorus of ohs and ahh's and several flower folk spread their petals wide, preening under my attention. Just being among them was lightening my spirits and my mouth twitched. Itching to smile freely. Nothing gave buttercups more pride than knowing they had elicited joy or gladness from another, but my kind weren't meant for such things and even out here, so far from court, prying eyes might report back.

"I would offer a smile in exchange for your wisdom. Is it a bargain?" A dozen chattering voices burst from the field, and they nodded emphatically. "I am searching for Ajisai Antor, leader of the Satyr Clan. Can you tell me how close I am?" A cacophony of tiny voices rose, making each impossible to understand. "Fair folk, I beg you, choose one to speak on your behalf and all will be rewarded."

The buttercup in my palm cleared her throat, and the others quieted, small black eyes blinking up at me. "You are closer than you think, but beware the skink." I stiffened. Skink worm thread. I'd seen what happened to those caught in a satyr's trap. One of my spies took six hours to unwind from the sticky stuff. "A bar of light, a glowing sign. Cross it, and secrets won't be thine."

I mulled her words over. The bar was unclear. I wanted to ask more, but a bargain was a bargain. I set the buttercup down among her inflorescence and stood. Stretching my lips wide, I gave them all my best smile. It was strange on my face, my cheeks growing sore nearly instantly, but the grove hummed in delight, their joyful magic rushing me, knitting some of the ache in my chest and I backed up, fearful my face would stick, the grin never leaving it.

Weaving through moss covered roots and mushroom-capped earth, it was dark when I reached a place at the edge of the Easter Wood. None dared enter the dark forest. Though its name suggested cheer and lightness, it was anything but and it was the one place in Faerie none of my waters had infiltrated. Once, the Easter Wood had been part of Spring, but centuries ago, in a battle between Spring and Autumn, the most famous dryad—believed to have been a goddess, like Luna and Gaia—gave her life to slow a troll attack that would have ended Spring.

When the arrow struck her heart, a black poison leached into the land, infecting everything, spreading over the border, into Autumn and killing all where they stood. But the poison didn't end there, killing trees, folk and creatures alike.

Most now believed you wouldn't die if you set foot in the Easter Wood, so many centuries later, but none were brave enough to risk it.

I wrapped my cloak more tightly around myself, edging along dark, twisted roots of dead bark, careful not to step on the infected land.

Whether I accepted the stories or not, it was an unnecessary risk. Rain began, infusing me with new energy, and I picked up speed, putting more distance between me and the putrid forest.

When darkness made it impossible to see, I gave up hope of finding the satyr clan this night and settled back against a mossy root to rest.

Soft yellow light hummed to life and whizzed past my head, disappearing into the fog. I craned my neck, straining to see where it had gone when another appeared and zipped away after the first. *FireFlies!*

I climbed to my feet as two more circled me and disappeared. Giving chase, I moved silently, knowing the satyrs would have lookouts near their camp.

Pressing a hand against a massive ash trunk, I peered around it and froze. Before me, the misty night was illuminated by an orange line of FireFlies. "A bar." I whispered.

"Indeed it is," a voice said beside me, and I spun around.

CHAPTER 14

Sav

Heavy lids cracked open, and I blinked against the light until the room swam into focus. My heart pounded in my ears, dragging me back to that night—when I'd woken after my first true encounter with Prince Fero.

But no. This time, the fault was mine alone.

Pain cleaved through my skull, sharp enough to draw a groan from my throat. I groped for a pillow and pressed it over my eyes, desperate to shut out the world.

The mattress dipped. My eyes flew open, the pillow tumbling from my grasp. I twisted, gaze snapping right.

"Morning, sleepyhead."

A loud woosh of air escaped me. "Mira. For a second there..."

She laughed. "Thought I was the handsome prince?"

I rolled over, burying my face in the pillow. "There's nothing handsome about him," I mumbled into my blankets.

"It didn't look mutual. He stared at you all night like you were his next meal."

I laughed, then let out another groan. "Don't make me laugh. Please."

A bell rang, and I covered my head with blankets.

The door creaked open. "Yes, Miss?"

"Might we have some water?" Mira asked.

"And spadeleaf," I called from under the covers.

The door burst open, and I uncovered my head. "What are you still doing in bed?" Sage demanded, storming in and ripping the blankets off. A chill bit into my bare arms and legs, goosebumps peppering my skin.

"Sage, get out!"

"We have luncheon with the prince and his brother. You have an obligation to be there." Sage paced away from me. "Why did you make such a fool of yourself last night?" She marched back to the bed. "Both of you."

Mira grabbed the blanket off the floor, wrapping it around herself. Sage reached for the edge, yanking hard, but Mira was much stronger, and Sage fell onto the bed. Red-faced, she shoved herself up. Mira exploded into a fit of giggles, and I laughed with her.

Sage tugged her skirts down, and lifting her fingers to her head, straightened a delicate silver circlet I hadn't seen buried in her curls. "It isn't funny. I will be a princess. You're my sister." Her gaze swiveled to Mira. "You're an emissary." As she ranted, she fought her curls to unwrap them from the crown she'd given herself.

Our laughter only grew louder, and Sage's cheeks flamed red. Letting out an exasperated huff, she ripped the silver circlet from her head, threw it on the floor and marched out of the room.

Mira climbed out of bed, lifting the delicate metal and placing it atop her head. A giggle was poised to escape my lips when she imitated my sister, but she sobered, eyes moving to the vanity mirror. "I'll never get to wear one of these."

I sat up, laying a hand on her arm. "Mira."

She smiled, sliding it off her head. "That's okay. I'd have to marry someone like Prince Sneezeweed. I'd rather be an emissary."

I snorted. "Prince Helenium, you mean?"

"Same thing."

I'd known the prince of Autumn might come, but with everything else going on, I'd nearly forgotten. When an enormous moose marched into the ballroom and shifted into the widest male I'd ever seen—naked, no less—we were all forced to bear witness before two Autumn Court attendants raced in with a burgundy cloak. And of course, he cut off Alder's speech to do it.

I should have been offended on behalf of my court, but I just raised my glass and laughed.

From there, the night descended into chaos.

After my fourth glass of henbane wine, the night grew fuzzy.

"You and the moose would make cute babies." Mira smirked. I grabbed a pillow lobbing it at her head. "Although I guess we'll never know how that love story ends since Prince Fero chased everyone who came near you off with a look."

A cold stone settled in my stomach. That much I remembered. Dark images, smudged at the edges, danced in my mind. Prince Fero had approached me several times throughout the night. I didn't remember why we hadn't danced, but I was fairly certain I had done nothing to embarrass the family. The night he'd pried my name from my lips raced to the forefront of my mind, making me nauseous. There was no telling what he would have commanded me to do in that state.

"But it could have been worse," Mira went on, oblivious to my inner turmoil. I hadn't shared my secret with her, and it seemed her brother hadn't either. "If my brother had come, he would have monopolized all your time. I like it better when it's just us."

My lips tugged up, but nausea roiled in my gut, swimming in a dizzying circle. What if he had done something? What if I couldn't remember? The room spun. I tasted bile. Then I tipped sideways and retched. Dark liquid spilled over the side of the bed, soaking a thick woven rug, staining it the color of blood.

I sat up, wiping my mouth. "Water. Mira."

"On it!" She bounced off the bed, unsettling my stomach once more, and I pressed a hand to my mouth, attempting to hold it down. It was no use. It was churning again, and I tipped sideways, leaning farther off the bed, as my dinner rushed up my esophagus, splattering across the cream rug.

That would stain.

"I'm here, Miss! Take this." I sat back in the bed, stretching trembling fingers for the cup. "Let me." A fawn dressed in an attendant's attire, lifted the glass to my lips and tipped it.

Cool liquid filled my mouth, washing away the taste of sour wine and stomach acid. I drank greedily, relishing the feeling as it swam in my calming stomach, leaching into my veins and washing away the remnants of last night's mistakes.

Mira stormed into the room, two full cups in hand, and I took one, steadier this time. The fawn who had attended me backed up.

"Wait!" I called. "I'm so sorry about the mess...."

"Rosemary, miss. Don't worry. I have magic that will take those stains right out." She smiled, her speckled velvety ear twitching as she dipped into a bow.

No, I groaned internally. No bowing. I wasn't a royal. No one should bow to me. Before I could correct her though, she was gone.

"Drink up. I don't want to spend today listening to Sage lecture us. Plus, the cute male who danced with me last night will be there," Mira said as she dropped back onto the bed beside me.

I sat up, finishing my second glass of water. The henbane was nearly gone, and my headache with it. Memories began filtering in. "Wait. Mira. It's not a good idea."

She swallowed the last of her water, glancing at me. "Why not? He's handsome. And tall. It's so hard to find a male taller than I am. Unless I want to date an orc." She grimaced.

"He's a Hawthorn. Don't waste your time on him."

When Mira and I had brushed our hair and dressed, we drifted down the main hall. While most of Spring's castle was a maze, the long central corridor was a straight line. For those unwilling to get lost in the labyrinth, one could always find their way in the hall. The one major drawback—the wall of blooms.

I squeezed against Mira's side, staring straight ahead. Perhaps if I didn't make eye contact, they wouldn't give my secret away. Mira gawked at them wide-eyed and jabbed me in the ribs. "Sav. Look. They're nearly bursting."

"Come on," I urged, dragging her forward.

At the end of the hall, Prince Fero stepped out of a room, eyes tracking immediately to the shriveled blackening blooms. I stilled my trembling fingers, squeezing them into fists. *Of all the fae to witness our trek through the flora.*

He pushed off the frame of his door, marching toward us.

Lengthening my stride, I turned, dragging Mira with me, and we nearly collided with Foxglove Hawthorn.

"Ladies." He dipped his chin and stepped back to give us room.

Not looking back to see if Prince Fero was behind us, I released Mira's arm and rushed to sit in a chair beside my sister. She narrowed her eyes, giving me a once-over, clearly unimpressed with my wardrobe choice. I looked down, smoothing my citrine gown. I had hoped it would please my sister to see me in pastels even if they clashed with my skin, but it seemed nothing would raise me in her estimation today.

I glanced over a shoulder, frowning at Mira who at stopped in the doorframe, now twirling a dark nail around an indigo tendril of hair, whispering to Foxglove. Her expression gave everything away. Foxglove's, by contrast, was unreadable—his face a perfect mask.

"Mira. Sit by me." I patted the seat beside me.

She blinked, gaze darting to me and then back to Foxglove.

Harmless dancing was one thing, but Mira's flirtation was dangerous. Her secret bloodline couldn't be exposed, not here. Not to him.

Drunken revelry was expected of water folk. Emotions, feelings toward another—were not.

I slid my chair back, preparing to intervene when Prince Fero stepped through the door and cleared his throat. All eyes turned to him, Mira and Foxglove breaking apart to give him space.

"I request a word with Lady Briar."

Beside me, my sister stilled, her hand hovering over a butter knife. Alder's gaze flicked to her, a deep V marring his brow. "What business can you have with my betrothed?"

"Pardon the confusion," Prince Fero said. "I meant the other Lady Briar."

All eyes swiveled to me. I straightened, lifting my chin, but before I could reply, my sister spoke.

"Of course, Prince. She would be delighted."

Under the table, a butter knife jabbed my thigh, and I bit down on an angry response. Who did she think she was, commanding me? My future princess, and that gave her every right. My stomach sank, and I searched in vain for Primrose. I wouldn't ask Mira to face that shark with me, but Primrose was a member of the royal family. Surely, Prince Fero wouldn't risk war with Spring.

But she was nowhere to be found. Come to think of it, last night I hadn't seen her after her dance with the prince of Autumn. I'd been too drunk to notice then, but a tendril of fear snaked up my spine now. What did it mean that she had disappeared after that dance and wasn't here this morning?

"Lady." Prince Fero had moved and was standing over me, towering like my executioner come to bring me to my end.

I squeezed trembling fingers under the table, steeling myself for the battle of wits that was sure to follow, and slid my hand into his. Standing, I let him lead me from the room. Mira watched me go, terror in her round eyes, but I subtly shook my head. Thankfully, she didn't follow. I hadn't told her my secret, and that was surely the only reason she hadn't insisted on joining us.

She feared a proposal or a tryst in the gardens. Not a male who could bend my will, snap it simply by saying my true name.

Prince Fero led me down the main corridor, striding confidently through the wall of blooms. They hissed and sparked, melting to dust as he passed. I glanced over a shoulder, gaping at the blackened wall he left in his wake. My knees wobbled, then buckled. He caught me easily, steadying me and giving me a once-over before saying nothing and continuing through the arched stone, toward the hedge maze.

We stopped beside the maze, and I exhaled a slow breath to steady my heart. Even as the fear threatened to consume rational thought, a flicker of warmth pooled in my belly, heating my blood. It answered the impending threat, rising to meet it. A new fear burst to life in me. Should this male learn my secret—my real secret—I did not know what he would do with it.

I shoved it down begging the fire climbing up my back to cool.

He released me, and I nearly tumbled to my knees. Will alone held me upright.

"This is familiar, is it not?"

His words were distant against the shouting in my mind, the torrent of pleas for my magic to remain dormant.

"What?"

"This is the maze I sent you to the night of the last ball. The night you met Primrose instead of me."

My mind was twisted with confusion.

He cleared his throat. "I must apologize."

"Sorry—what?" The word slipped out again. Mab, was I a parrot now?

"I should not have used your name against you. I should not have asked for it. It's my innate gift. You're so young. I hadn't expected to need to guard against the use of my magic."

What! screamed in my brain. *What?* What was he saying? What did his words mean? They were a jumble in my mind, and I couldn't make them out. This was a trick. The moment before he brought the knife out to gut me.

"In truth, I've never felt such powerful magic in another."

Alarm bells drowned all rational thought. Feel magic? He can feel my magic? All fae could perceive it—somewhat. And those as powerful as Fero couldn't help it occasionally when it seeped out, drenching those around them. But a magic sensor. Rare. So rare. And extremely dangerous.

In a principality where power determined your station, his gift made him a threat. Suddenly, I wondered if any others in Summer had met an untimely end before they could be tested. I backed up. I was likely only alive because I was in Spring and had no claim to his throne. Would that stop him? Or was he bent on eradicating all competition? I nearly choked on a hysterical laugh. As powerful as him? Was I losing my mind?

Heat sizzled in my veins. It would seek an outlet soon. Protection at all costs. Its only goal was to ensure I survived whatever this was, and his magic was enough to destroy an army. Red tinged the edges of my vision.

"Lady Briar. I have tried to seek you out since that night. To promise that I will never do something like that again. But also to warn you."

His words were a bucket of ice dumped over me. Smoke poured from my nostrils, and I gasped, stumbling backward.

The prince's eyes went wide. "Fascinating."

"I—" My words were cut off as puffs of white choked my throat, and I coughed, gagging on the thick smoke. I turned, tripping in the fog of my own making—then ran.

CHAPTER 15

Kaspar

T he skink worm thread clung like tar, resisting every twist of my wrists. It was no use. I didn't have the wild fae magic it would take to free myself of these bindings.

The satyr had tied my hands in the dark before I ever saw her face. Now she grinned like we were old friends and beckoned me forward. The second—the one I'd never seen coming—jabbed a spear in my back, leaving no room for argument.

I glanced up as we stopped at the base of an enormous ash tree. In the canopy. Of course. I'd traveled the woods of Faerie a hundred times but never thought to search the branches overhead. My world was below and theirs was above.

"Climb, Kelpie," the satyr at my back commanded.

I held up my bound wrists. "A difficult task, don't you think?"

Her sharp spear dug into my spine, and I winced.

"Enough Scortcha. Release him." A satyr appeared from the darkness, golden eyes gleaming. Her gilded hair shimmered in the FireFly light, coiled with horns that looped overhead like a crown. Power radiated from her in waves, ancient and wild.

"But."

"But nothing, Scortcha. Do you know who our guest is?"

"Kelpie scum." Scortcha spat at my feet.

"This is a prince, a powerful one. And if he had wanted it, he could have drowned us all where we stood, bound wrists or no." She turned her gaze on me. "He is not here in search of a fight. Are you, Prince of Lakes and Streams?"

I shook my head. This satyr was growing in my esteem by the moment. "I'm seeking Ajisai Antor, leader of this clan."

The satyr waved a hand, and my sticky bonds vanished. "You've found her. What can I do for you, Prince?"

When we had climbed to the home high in the treetops, and I had explained the issue, leaving out Sav's identity, Ajisai nodded gravely. "You must know we do not concern ourselves with the goings-on of the fae courts."

"I do, but there are things at play that affect all of Faerie. You know the power Fero wields. Power that great might destroy us all. Can we afford another war like the one that destroyed the Easter Wood?"

"What makes you so sure he will use this fae you mentioned in such a way?"

"He has her true name."

A gasp from the satyr behind Ajisai. She glanced over a shoulder, giving the warrior a disapproving shake of her head. Returning her focus to me, she folded her hands in her lap. "Better we rid Faerie of such a creature."

"You can't think you could take down Fero."

"I mean the fire fae."

My throat dried. This satyr might learn Sav's identity and end her should these talks go badly. A clan of trained warriors would be difficult to defend against.

"Why take a life when we can diminish her power? Surely death isn't the best option."

Ajisai's golden brow rose, and she cocked her head. "I see. This is a personal matter."

I relaxed my posture, slouching against a tree branch at my back. "You assume a great deal about a sea fae. When is a matter ever personal to one of my kind?" I kept my face blank.

A grumble of assent from the satyrs stung a little, but in this moment, I'd never been more grateful to rely on our kind's reputation. Should she suspect this was a plea from the heart and not a practical one, it might mean Sav's death.

"What then does the court of Lakes and Streams gain by allowing the creature to live?"

I pictured a gentle stream flowing over rocks, steady, soothing, strong. The burbling current forced my fear for Sav from my mind. I exhaled slowly through my nose, willing my pulse to follow the water's calm rhythm. "My neighboring court is my greatest ally. She has already captured Summer's attention. Should she die, they would take it as an act of war." I glanced down at my nails. "A war between my neighbors brings blood to my door."

Ajisai's glimmering eyes pierced me, and it felt as though her gaze burned all my walls to ash, leaving my bleeding heart raw and exposed.

"Very well. We have a tonic that will suppress her magic. It lasts only a moon cycle. You'll need to slip it in her drink at each crescent moon."

I counted to three before nodding slowly. The stream in my mind flowed glacially, soothing my rapid pulse. This news was the answer to all my troubles, but I couldn't risk the satyrs knowing how much it mattered to me. If Sav were believed to be weak, she would be forgotten by her family and those at court who only desired power. I exhaled a steadying breath through my nose.

Ajisai snapped her fingers. "Juniper. Bring me the Amanita Verna tea."

A satyr with the same golden curls and eyes as Ajisai climbed down a thick branch, dropping beside us, glaring at me. "Ammi. Give it to him instead," she said in thickly accented elvish. My shoulders stiffened. She'd chosen the common tongue to ensure I understood the threat.

"Hush, Juniper." Ajisai narrowed her eyes at the satyr. "Forgive my daughter; she is not overly fond of your sex."

I had heard rumors that satyrs killed their boys, keeping only one alive for breeding in any given clan. I wasn't entirely sure it was a lie. Since entering their camp, I'd only seen females. Fearsome creatures—strapped to the hilt in shining weapons—guarded their tree, keen eyes watching for any threat.

I swallowed. It had been unwise to make this trip without doing more research on the reclusive folk first, but time was not on my side, and I didn't trust Mira to aid Sav should her magic slip through again. I rose to my feet, and several females reached for their weapons.

"I offer my gratitude for this gift, Ajisai." I dipped my head, holding out my palm to Juniper.

She snapped sharp teeth at my fingers. I held my hand steady. To flinch would be a weakness. She lifted her lip, growling at me, but after a moment, when I hadn't moved, she dropped a small pouch in my palm.

I turned to leave, but Ajisai's words stopped me. "We will require more than your gratitude, I'm afraid."

CHAPTER 16

Sav

Mira found me in the baths and I kicked myself for forgetting her. If anyone was more alone in this court than me, it was Mira. At least I had a sister. She sunk into a tub beside me grinning contentedly. "I needed this."

I glanced over, watching the scales erupt along her arms and chest, forming armor we land fae didn't have. A foe would need a great deal of strength to pierce them.

We sat in silence for some time. There was another party tonight. Another event to dress for, but the afternoon was surprisingly void of responsibilities. The water, though warm, cooled my heated veins, and did an amazing job of regulating my internal temperature. I daydreamed of spending the night here, soaking until my toes were wrinkled, but Sage would never forgive me.

Some of the tension crept back into my limbs as the summer prince's words ran through my mind for the dozenth time. I still didn't understand what he meant. How had he used my gift against me? I couldn't worry about that now. The real danger was what he knew and what he

might do with it. Secrets weren't just currency in his hands. They were weapons.

"Do you think Foxglove will ask me to dance tonight?"

I opened my eyes, glancing over at Mira. "Oh Mira. I'd prefer you flirt with anyone but him."

She narrowed her eyes. "What do you have against him? Upset he's not falling all over himself for you like the other males?"

"No," I scoffed. "He's the prince's brother. There's something wrong with the whole family. Alder killed his advisors when he took the throne."

Mira shrugged. "Just because they're related, doesn't make them the same. Look at you and Sage."

"We're twins. Two fae couldn't be more alike." Mira snorted, sounding suspiciously like a horse and I laughed with her. "Okay, we have some differences."

She rolled her eyes. "You think?"

I splashed water over the rim of my tub, spraying it across her face.

She sat up, flicking a wrist and a wall of water crashed over me. I sputtered, and choked, wiping my eyes. "No fair," I gasped.

"You know, for a fae with so many water folk for friends you'd think you could do a better job holding your breath."

Running a hand down my deep emerald gown, I glanced at the sparkling jewels Sage had sent to my room. They were extravagant; too much for a girl from a village at the edge of her province. Had Sage not been destined to wed the prince, I may have been a healer, like Ivy, or found work in some other simple profession.

Not if Father had anything to say about it, though.

If Sage hadn't been promised to Alder, mother would have found some other noble to marry her off to. *Mother.* The one good thing about all the time we'd been spending in court was the break from father's tears. Guilt twisted in my gut at my lack of empathy. Truly, I longed for a love like theirs. For a male to mourn me forever if we should be parted, but even after so long, Father showed no signs of recovering. Perhaps a love so great was more of a curse than a blessing.

I lifted the sparkling choker to my throat, reaching around the back of my neck to clasp it and clipped the pair of gold tips over the tops of my pointed ears. They sparkled in the low light and I turned my head from side to side admiring them. Most of the time I found Sage's obsession with dressing up silly, but every now and then, I enjoyed the finer things that came with her new station.

A soft knock sounded at my door and I turned. "Enter."

Primrose's sandy curls spilled into the room and her eyes met mine.

"Primrose!" I raced to the door, clasping her hands. "I was worried for you." Her smile didn't reach her eyes. My stomach dropped. "What is it?"

"I'm sorry for missing luncheon. I was in no mood."

She moved into my room, and we sat at the edge of my bed. "Tell me."

"I'm to marry."

"Kaspar? But how?"

Mab would never allow it. But if anyone could convince our queen, it was my friend. If they wed, I would celebrate them, visit them often. A twinge of sadness, knowing I was to lose a friend I'd only just gained, stung, but I brushed it aside. Their happiness was what mattered most.

But it wasn't happiness I saw in her eyes.

"It's not Kaspar?"

She shook her head, tears brimming in her eyes. "Prince Helenium." She choked on his name and buried her head in my hair. "Foxglove tried to intercede on my behalf, but Alder won't hear it. He wants an alliance with Autumn, and it seems I will be the cost."

My arms were numb as they wrapped around Prim's shaking shoulders. "There's a chance Mab won't agree to it."

A sob escaped Primrose. "Mab has already agreed. Autumn's seer has predicted our union will bring centuries of peace between Spring and Autumn. It was all the persuading Mab needed."

I hugged my friend tighter, holding her while she cried. Once, I'd imagined Sage and I being this kind of close, comforting each other when Father or Uncle forced us to marry. I was surprised to find myself comforting a female I'd only known a few weeks. "I'm sorry, Prim."

"I knew this day would come." She lifted her head, wiping a hand across her cheeks. "The one bright spot in all of this is that we are forbidden from bearing children. It will be my excuse to limit my duties in his bedroom."

I stiffened.

Imagining the ruddy-cheeked male, who was nearly as wide as he was tall, pinning the fair-haired female down, made heat simmer in my veins, magic surging with it. My hands curled into fists, nails cutting crescent moons into my palms.

Not now. Not here. Prim couldn't see this.

Thoughts clawed at me. Our court's history; every memory of how males used their strength and power to grind females down. The injustice set my blood aflame, and with it, my magic. If Prim sensed it, if she guessed what I was hiding...

I forced air through my nose, dragging the heat back down, burying it beneath my ribs.

"At least in Autumn you'll be free to visit me," I managed, voice tight with the effort, "and it's truly a blessing for Spring to have Autumn as our ally."

Primrose sniffled. "You're right about the second part. I am honored to do this for Spring. You must visit me. Often." She wiped her cheeks. "He's just so old."

I inhaled a steady breath. "Perhaps he'll die soon."

Primrose laughed through her tears and leaned into me again. We stayed like that until Mira arrived in another sparkling gown, cut low, exposing her back.

"Were you gossiping without me?" she demanded, throwing her arms around us both.

I untangled myself from our trio.

"Come. Let us celebrate while we all still have our freedom."

CHAPTER 17

Kaspar

Tucking the pouch in my pocket, I hopped the distance from the tree to the ground, shifted, and galloped away. I'd already lingered too long in satyr territory. It had been three days since I had left my sister and Sav to fend for themselves among the court vipers.

Wasting no time on surprise, I raced over spongy earth, not slowing until it had become grass underfoot.

That had been my first encounter with the golden-eyed leader of the satyrs, and I didn't look forward to our next. I had six months of tea. Enough to get Sav through her testing ceremony. That gave me half a year to come up with a plan before our next meeting. A satyr's bargain was as ironclad as any other fae, but I had time to find leverage. Time to give Ajisai a reason to dissolve our agreement.

Once Sav turned twenty-five and the world saw her magic, she wouldn't need protection. She'd be untouchable—even to me. That thought lodged sharp and bitter beneath my ribs, and I drove my hooves harder into the earth, as if outrunning it might stop it from being true. But princes had many enemies, and I was no exception. I had been selfish

to make our acquaintance so public. To paint a target on her back. That ended now.

I reached the stream in late afternoon and dove in. In my shifted form, my weight carried me easily to the bottom, and I raced along the bed. Funneling a current through my veins, I pushed faster than any other water folk could—apart from my uncle—and above, the stream became a raging river. It sloshed over the earth, washing away grass and debris as it expanded far beyond the bounds of the small border separating Spring and Autumn. I didn't care. Didn't give thought to the tiny creatures who might be crushed in my power's wake. I cared only for my destination, even knowing each moment I drew closer was a moment closer to severing my connection with Sav forever.

It was just after midnight when I arrived at the edge of Spring Court. Rain sluiced over my bare skin, a balm after days without rest, and I pushed faster toward the castle. After so many nights without sleep, I needed the energy. The rain restored me, and I moved faster. At the arched entry to Spring, two guards stepped aside as velvet slacks, a turquoise top, and a velvet coat materialized from my closet.

The lilting hum of music tugged me forward, begging me to join the revelry of a ball already in progress. I shook my head, pasting the icy look I donned for the world on my face as I stepped through the doors, scanning the crowd.

A mane of auburn hair, styled with two glittering combs swung around the dance floor, and my blood ran cold. On her arm, the prince of Summer smiled when she tipped back in his arms. She came up, a grin splitting her face, and I saw red. She laughed, easy and open, the sound crashing over me like a wave. The room tilted. I felt it in my spine, in the base of my throat.

I cut straight for them, knocking folk aside. A few grumbled before realizing who I was and began clearing a path.

Mira stepped in front of me. "Prince Kaspar, welcome back."

"Move."

Fae glanced our way, making no pretense of hiding their interest.

"I believe your highness needs a drink."

"*Your* Highness demands you get out of my way."

Mira laughed high and fake, setting a hand on my arm. "Perhaps one before whatever urgent business brought you to court?"

I glanced at the orc guards lining the walls. No soldier of Spring's would dare lay a hand on me, but Mira's warning had reminded me, an act against another court's sovereign, especially in public, would be a declaration of war. One I wasn't prepared to wage, even for Sav's sake.

I exhaled a calming breath, loosening my shoulders. "Too right, Emissary. Drink with me and catch me up on all that has occurred in my absence."

Mira nodded, understanding my meaning, and took my arm. We moved to the low tables at the back of the ballroom, and I snatched a glass, downing it in one go. Mira lifted her glass to her lips, smiling at the fae still watching us. I had no doubt several were trained, as my spies were, to read lips, but I didn't need to warn my sister.

Glass still pressed to her mouth, she pitched her voice so only I could hear. "Whatever is happening between you and Sav, she welcomed his attention this night. Don't make a fool of yourself."

I swiped another glass from the table, bringing it to my mouth. "There are things you don't understand. She cannot be alone with him."

"They're in a ballroom full of folk. I'd hardly call it alone."

A growl rumbled up my throat. I sipped the dark liquid, vision blurring more from lack of sleep than wine, though I rarely drank. A clear mind was the best weapon, but tonight, I was already muddled. What was one more thing to distract me?

My gaze drifted over the room, and I worked to avoid the redhead at its center, having a grand time with a male she was supposed to fear. Spring's emissary was crowded against a wall, face pale, and my attention snapped to her. The gray-haired male pinning her there dwarfed her. There was no mistaking the prince of Autumn.

I set my glass down. "Stay here."

Mira followed my gaze and downed her glass, setting it beside mine before following after. I looked back. "I asked you not to come."

"You're not in charge of me."

I fought the urge to roll my eyes when so many gazes were heavy on me. "Truly I am in every sense of the word."

Clearing my throat behind Prince Helenium, I squared my shoulders. He spun around, bleary-eyed. "What is it?"

His rasping tone set my teeth on edge, but I dipped my chin in deference to his age alone. "May I steal the lady for a moment?"

He frowned, but his gaze darted past me, trailing the length of my sister, and I moved to block his view.

Primrose pushed off the wall, grabbing my hand and nearly running for the dance floor. I wrapped my fingers around Mira's wrist, pulling her with us. On our way to the center of the room, Lord Hawthorn, the younger brother, stepped into my path.

"Excuse me, I'd like the honor of a dance with your emissary."

"No." I marched past him, dragging Mira behind me. She pulled hard against my hold, and I glanced back at her.

Turquoise lips were pinched tightly, and her brows were low. She'd had enough of me, and I saw in her face it would be a fight in a moment. My sister's erratic temper, especially when it came to me, could not be controlled. I released her. "Go. Dance with him. One dance."

Her expression smoothed into one of triumph, and she dashed away without another word. I'd need to keep a closer eye on whatever was happening there, but at the moment I had other concerns to attend to. Ones that required a dance partner.

Spinning onto the floor, the music wrapped around us, lightening our steps, and soon Lady Magnolia and I were among the dancing revelers. Her eyes sparkled, and her shoulders relaxed as she leaned into me. Some of my tension eased. If I were forced to continue using her to draw attention from my erratic emotions, at least I could bring her some measure of joy.

I'd brushed off the confession I'd overheard her tell Sav as just another court flirtation. But maybe she was the cover I needed. We whirled, coming closer to the prince and his partner, and Sav beamed when she saw me. "Glad you're back," she mouthed as they spun by us.

A hand touched my cheek, turning my face to Primrose's, and she gave me a devilish grin as her fingers slid down my chest. They traced the outline of my cock, and my eyes widened as she cupped my balls, pulling me closer. I bit the inside of my cheek to keep from swearing as my gaze shot up, but Sav had already twirled away, caught up in the music and her partner.

Mira appeared beside us, and I looked up at the couple, understanding what had drawn her to him. They were a pair of giraffes. My sister's lips tipped up, eyes dreamy, and my heart warmed. When was the last time a male had made her smile? Had my court known what she was to me, no doubt she would have plenty of eager males in her bed; all the more reason for them to be left in the dark. Mira deserved something real. With someone who wouldn't use her as they did all royals. It wouldn't be a Hawthorn, but she deserved this moment to bask in someone's attention.

Primrose pressed her lips to my ear. "You're very sweet to your subjects." She ran her tongue over the ridge and up to the tip of my ear.

I leaned back, putting a little distance between us, and gave her a lazy grin. I had no issue with willing company, but Primrose wanted more than I could give.

The sparkle in her eyes dimmed when she met my gaze. "You *do* love her."

A bolt of ice shot down my spine, and I nearly lost my step. My spine stiffened. A single beat passed. I couldn't let her see it. Not even for a moment. Recovering quickly, I relaxed my grip around her waist. "You're mistaken, Lady. Water folk don't feel such things."

"Then a night with me is unappealing for other reasons?"

I fought my every desire to glance at the fae who was the reason no strings would be the only thing I offered any male or female. I let my gaze trail her, lingering on her breasts, trying and failing not to compare them to the creature who owned me. "Not at all."

Primrose swayed with the music and on the next spin, twisted in my arms, pressing her lips to mine. I let her linger—tried to convince myself it didn't matter. When she opened her eyes, heat burned in them. "Come on." She spun us off the dance floor, pulling me toward the door.

A shout behind us made me turn in time to see Mira slap Foxglove hard across the face. His expression was a mask of fury, and I tugged my hand out of Primrose's, crossing the room. Mira crashed into me, tears spilling down her cheeks. Rage boiled my veins, and I wrapped an arm around her. A moment of terror doused the anger as I glanced around at all the eyes on Mira, widened in surprise.

Water folk didn't cry. Didn't make scenes. Panic twisted through me, sharp and breathless. If anyone realized what Mira's tears meant, she'd be hunted like prey. Everyone was looking now. Watching my sister melt. Watching me to see what I would do. Sav spun to a stop, reaching for Mira and tugged her away, leaving Foxglove standing before me.

"What insult have you leveled on my court, Lord Hawthorn?" I fought the anger, wrestling it into calculating calm.

"It was a misunderstanding. If you would allow me to speak with her. To make amends."

He moved, but I was faster, sucking the air from his lungs. Glasses rattled on the table as all the moisture in the room begged me to command it. To unleash my wrath on the male who offended my sister.

Foxglove dropped to his knees, gasping for air that would not come.

"Gentlefolk, perhaps we take this outside."

My gaze swiveled to Prince Fero, and a fresh rush of power surged in my veins, begging for release. His magic prodded mine, testing for a way to break my hold over the fae turning purple on the floor. It only incited my rage.

"What is the meaning of this!" Prince Alder shouted, appearing on my right.

"Your court has offended my emissary." I leveled Alder with a withering glare.

"My guards tell me it was your emissary who struck my brother."

A wall of heat crashed over me, breaking my hold on Foxglove and sending me to my knees. Several orc guards rushed forward, but Prince Fero held up a hand, and a gasp escaped the crowd when they obeyed.

"Take him!" Alder screamed, but the orcs stood rigid and slowly, the pressure lifted.

I staggered to my feet as the summer prince withdrew his magic. Foxglove held a hand to his throat, glaring daggers at me. The guards all watched me closely, hands on weapons should I make another move. Only Alder was still blubbering commands. No one listened, of course. Even his own guards had learned to tune him out.

I turned, storming from the room.

In the long corridor outside the ballroom, Sav held Mira, and thankfully her cheeks were dry.

"We're leaving," I said, not waiting for Mira to follow.

Whispered words chased me down the hall. I stopped at the arched entry to Spring's castle, turning. Mira gave Sav a final hug before shifting into kelpie form and galloping down the hall. I followed her lead, welcoming the change. We raced through the gardens toward home, my magic still simmering in my chest, and my heart somewhere behind me on the ballroom floor.

CHAPTER 18

Sav

I watched them go, dread curling low in my gut. If Kaspar had waited—if he'd listened—maybe he wouldn't have lit the fuse. But for all his restraint, an offense to anyone in his court was war. And tonight, he was both prince and brother.

In the silence that followed, I heard a noise I couldn't place. It was almost as if... I broke into a run, rounding a corner and froze. Prince Helenium's rotund frame blocked most of my view. Only meaty hands wrapped around Primrose's slender throat were visible. She gurgled, eyes bulging in their sockets.

"Stop!" I screamed, racing forward.

A hand swung for me and I was flung to the ground. I jumped to my feet, pounding fists against his thick arms, but he ignored me, squeezing the life from my friend.

"Stop!" I shouted again. Terror and fury burned inside me, blazing to life. I screamed, clutching his arm as fire burst from my palms, scorching everything it touched. The horrid scent of burning meat invaded my nostrils as his skin melted in my grasp and the prince stumbled back, releasing Primrose.

She crumpled to the floor, and I dropped beside her. Heat radiated from my fingertips, and I was afraid to touch her—to burn her—and see if she was still alive.

"Low-bred whore." Helenium's voice cracked like a whip before I felt the sharp jerk, my scalp screaming, as he yanked me off the floor.

I barely raised my hands before his fist cracked against my cheekbone, stars bursting behind my eyes. I slumped in his hold, but he didn't release my hair, swinging for my face again. Dazed, I closed my eyes, waiting for the next blow.

He shouted another insult, but the pain never came and the pressure on my scalp eased as his weight came down on top of me, suffocating me. I tried to yell, to shove him off, but I was trapped. Panic ripped through me. My hands trembled so hard I could barely feel my fingers, and before I could think, the fire burst from my palms—wild, feral—not something I called but something that wanted to be free, incinerating any part of him that touched me.

His weight rolled off and a scream burst from my lungs. Hands reached for me and I swiped at them, shooting balls of flame at my attacker.

"Sav. You're okay."

The words registered and the scene before me solidified. Prince Fero lifted me to a sitting position, searching my face. Behind him the outline of a round, lifelines body lay.

"What happened?"

"He would have killed you."

I nodded dumbly. I would have met Primrose's fate. "Primrose." I rolled onto my side, the world swaying dangerously and let out a soft whimper.

Primrose blinked bloodshot, swollen eyes, and a smile split her cracked lips. Dark purple was already beginning to mar her skin and I crawled to her, wrapping my arms around her. "He can't hurt you."

Tears leaked down her mottled, puffy cheeks and she touched a hand gingerly to her neck.

A clattering of feet sounded behind Prince Fero and I looked up. Prince Alder and his brother stood in the hall, flanked by several Spring Court guards.

"Prim!" Foxglove darted forward, scooping his cousin into his arms. I slumped into the wall, watching his back as he carried her away. To a healer I hoped.

"Arrest him." Prince Alder order.

General Creig stepped forward but Prince Fero held up a hand and he froze. I wasn't imagining the twinge of anger on the general's face. He was holding him at bay. As he likely had in the ballroom when they intended to arrest Kaspar. Why?

"I said, seize him!"

Prince Fero straightened. "You find yourself in a difficult situation, Prince of Spring. Your brother incited war with Lakes and Streams. Autumn attempted to kill your cousin and would have killed the sister of your bride. Will you make an enemy of a third principality in one night?"

"I will not be responsible for the war Autumn drags to your gates. All we have is your word. Prince Helenium cannot speak for himself."

Alder snapped his fingers. Nothing. The prince of Summer had yet to release Spring's guards, and they stood rigid as statues, eyes wide, breath caught in their throats.

Fero stepped over the charred remains of Helenium's body, stopping in front of Alder. He towered over my sister's fiancé, and my vision blurred as steam seemed to waft off him. He raised one hand, a ball of fire bursting to life in it. He raised the other and a ball of liquid formed, pulled from the very air.

"I am the most powerful fae in an age, wielder of fire and water, a dual gift unseen in centuries. Prince of the largest principality in all of Faerie. You have two choices tonight. Make an enemy of me. Or forget what you saw in this hall and leave Autumn to squabble amongst themselves."

Alder hadn't answered, but Fero had already decided.

General Creig and his men parted, whether out of respect or by force I would never know. He walked with an unhurried gait, and as he moved through the wall of blooms they burst into flames, the entire wall blackening and shriveling. When he reached the arched doors he turned, meeting my unfocused gaze and pursed his lips.

I stared back, trying and failing to puzzle him out. Had this all been a carefully orchestrated plan by a master strategist or had the male who saved our lives wished for peace?

When he'd gone, Alder stormed away, leaving a charred corpse—and me—behind.

The orc general dropped to one knee, holding out a hand. "Lady."

I stared up at his battle scarred face, finding only kindness in it. What he thought of the scene he'd found us in, or my part in it, I couldn't say. I slid my hand in his and he tugged me up. My heart beat erratically in my chest as I prepared for him to cart me to the dungeon for further questioning or possibly to rot, asking no questions at all.

For a desperate moment, we stood, staring at one another, my tongue sticky in my mouth.

His olive lips quirked up. "Let's get you to the healer."

"Use the spadeleaf sparingly. I know you and your sister like to lick the leaves."

I gasped in mock horror. "I have no idea what you mean." The jovial words scraped strangely on my tongue, foreign after the week I'd endured. Yet welcome, too. A reprieve from talking of politics. Or corpses.

Ivy rolled her eyes, one hand braced on her hip. "I was your age not so long ago. I remember what young fae get up to."

I offered her my most innocent smile as she pressed a jar of paste into my hands. I turned, pushing open her vined door. True to his word, Kaspar had helped Ferndell rebuild, and warmth flickered in my chest at the thought of his kindness.

A week had passed since the ball. Since Kaspar's departure with Mira. Since the death of Autumn's prince. Alder's missive to their court had called it a mystery, a matter under investigation, and he'd promised to share any truths we uncovered.

But Fero had not returned. I doubted he ever would. Whatever had drawn him to Spring, he had taken what he came for. Fear knotted deep in my chest. Too many now knew my secret. And with Sage's wedding looming two months away, Alder preparing his court for war with Kaspar, and Primrose's healing going slower than the palace physician liked, my thoughts frayed like threads pulled thin. One more tug, and I would unravel.

I left Ivy's home, following the well-worn path to my small cottage outside the village and pulled the door open. Sage looked up from her book. "Did you get it?"

I smiled, holding up the pot. At least at home, Sage and I were back to our normal selves, for the short time we had until she moved into the castle. "Yep."

"Good. I don't want you looking like a cyclops at my wedding."

I rolled my eyes. "It's two months away, Sage. I will be fully healed by then."

She stood, letting her book drop. I winced as the spine hit the floor with a thud. Not her book—mine. She didn't even notice. Just let it fall like it meant nothing. "Two weeks, not two months. Do you never listen to a word I say? My prince has moved up the wedding. He fears an attack."

I frowned, grimacing at the pain in my cheek. "Moving up the date doesn't change your birthday. What does he hope to gain by it?"

Sage huffed, ruffling the curls framing her face. Her hair always hung so neatly. It was unfair. But, she did take the time to roll it each night. Perhaps mine wouldn't be so wild if I spent a little time on it. I resolved myself to do just that when we moved into the palace. I would need to look the part of the princess's sister.

My gaze dropped to my abused book on the floor. When we moved, I would get a lock for my door so Sage couldn't sneak in to steal any more of my things.

"He thinks Prince Kaspar won't attack if it means attacking a friend."

I looked up. "Kaspar won't attack."

"Won't I?"

My sister and I turned toward the door as Kaspar stepped inside. I hovered on the balls of my feet. Normally I would go to him, throw my arms around him, but I wasn't sure how to greet the prince from a province we may be at war with. Where would I stand when the line was drawn between them? My sister was to be the princess. Spring was my home. My family's home. But Kaspar was my best friend.

His cool gaze surveyed my sister for a long moment before finding me. There was something coiled beneath his skin, a pressure in the air that made my stomach knot. Power, yes—but something colder too. Calculating.

"You will bring a message to your prince," he said, gaze darting back to Sage.

"What message?" Sage and I said in unison.

Kaspar closed the distance between us, lifting my fingers to his lips. "Princess."

Sage choked on a scoff. "You can't mean it."

I looked to my sister in confusion. "Mean what?"

Kaspar let my hand fall, dismissing me with a glance, and gave Sage his full attention. "Mira explained what happened. I understand my behavior may have come across as rash. The offense must be mended. What better way to do so than a marriage alliance?"

I backed up, bumping the table. "Kaspar, be serious."

He ignored me. "Will you take this message to your betrothed?"

"A simple apology is all that's needed." I demanded, pushing away from the table. "And you forget. No one has asked me."

"What do you think, Princess Hawthorn? Would your betrothed lay down arms... if I laid down a crown?"

I huffed, heat climbing up my spine. I was not a bargaining chip.

"I believe he would."

"No." I moved, blocking Kaspar's view of Sage and waved a hand in his face. "Kaspar. What are you doing? I will not marry you."

His eyes focused on me. Cold indifference brimming in a place I'd only ever seen kindness before. "Will you doom us to be enemies then? Will Spring and Lakes and Streams wage war, killing innocent lives until one side or the other cedes?"

"No, but—"

"Then it's done."

Could he have truly convinced Mab to allow such a thing? She'd agreed to Prim and Helenium's marriage. The heat creeping up my spine rushed to my heart, and I felt it. It was coming. I wouldn't be able to stop it. I hadn't told Sage. I had planned to, but with everything happening, we hadn't connected much these weeks and now she would find out by accident. When I burned our home to the ground.

She would never forgive me.

I tried to push it down, to cram it back into its box, but the idea of a forced marriage, one my best friend plotted, scorched my insides.

Kaspar's eyes widened and he grabbed my hand. "A moment." He yanked me behind him, pulling me out the door. His cool touch was doing little to sooth the fire inside, and tiny sparks flamed to life along my fingertips.

"Let me go. I'll burn you."

He released me. "Get to the lake. Don't let anyone see."

Panic seized me and the flames sparked off my palms. I ran and ran, racing into the forest, following the path I'd taken so many times to the lake, to my best friend. The betrayal was what hurt the most, and smoke curled from my nostrils, a warning I couldn't swallow. Faster. I had to go faster.

I reached the lake, diving in and exhaled a plume of bubbles as a small ripple of heat shot out, dissipating to nothing. For a moment, I floated, letting the cool liquid wash over my fiery skin. My mind cleared, some of the anger washing away and I considered Kaspar's words. I hadn't understood why Sage knew what he intended before I did.

Princess. He'd said it often enough that it lost meaning for me—but not for Sage. He'd used it like a dagger, carefully placed. He wanted her listening before I even understood the game. Had he counted on it inciting my emotion? Made me angry so it was clear I was the one unwilling and not him? *He had.* He had used me to mend the relationship between our two courts. I was only mildly relieved he didn't truly mean to marry me. The other ninety-percent of my brain was fuming all over again. He could have warned me. But maybe he didn't trust me to play along. Or worse, maybe he didn't care.

I should have known. Mab may have agreed to two land creatures marrying, but she would never agree to a marriage between land and sea. Though he did not need her permission, *I* certainly did.

A dark shape slid overhead, the water dispersing to make space for Kaspar as he sank beside me. I narrowed my eyes at him. He pointed to his mouth, then up. Giving me the option, His air or the air above. No way was I putting my lips anywhere near the manipulative bastard.

I kicked off the floor hard, breaking the surface with a gasp. The air felt thin after everything he'd taken.

He rose, head bobbing above the water and I envied his ease of floating, while I flailed like a dying fish to tread water.

"Come on."

"I'm not going anywhere with you."

"Mira wants to see you."

I hesitated. "Fine. But I know what you did."

His lips twitched. Just for a moment, I thought I'd see him smile.

CHAPTER 19

Kaspar

Sav sucked in a breath before wrapping herself around me, arms tight at my neck, legs cinched around my waist. The world above vanished in a rush of bubbles as I dove, and her body pressed hard to mine. Every inch of her warmth clashed with the cold pull of the sea, and the contrast left me raw.

I cut through the water, diving for the palace, but my thoughts weren't on the current or the magic burning in my veins. They were on her. The way her grip dug into my shoulders; the way she held on like I was the only thing keeping her from drowning. She belonged there. She always had.

We shot through a narrow cave, naiads turning curious faces as we passed. Let them stare. Let them whisper. They'd see their prince carrying what he wanted most in this world—and what he could never have.

Her legs tightened, and I nearly faltered. To feel her cling to me, to bring her home, was the sweetest torment I'd ever known.

On the slick stone floor she slid free as my tail split. "Kaspar, please."

"I'm putting on pants. Calm down." The words came out sharper than I meant, but her tone cut the ache in me clean in half. A reminder. She didn't feel the way I did.

"I'm still mad at you." Her brow pinched, trying for menace. But the freckles scattering across her nose ruined the effect, and I hated how much I adored it.

I bit down on the smile threatening to break loose. Her refusal still stung, though I'd counted on it. Even if she'd loved me, that proposal would have lit her temper on fire. I'd needed it to. When Sage reported my desperate attempt to mend the relationship, I knew Alder would agree to ally once more.

But Alder was weak until his bride sat the throne. And if I chose to, I could raze his court without lifting more than a hand. I never would. And that, more than anything, was the problem. Because if it came to war, the one thing I'd want to save, the one thing I'd take for myself, was the fae who would never forgive me for it.

"Sav!"

I turned just in time to see Mira crash into Sav, knocking her into the wall with a squeal.

Mira grinned, eyes shining. But just as quickly, her expression crumpled. That look—I recognized it. Hope, curdling into dread.

"It's horrible," she whispered, arms clinging tightly to Sav's. "He won't let me go back. I've told him a dozen times it was all a misunderstanding. I was drunk. Foxglove would never do anything to hurt me."

"Let her breathe, sister."

"Oh, I'm sorry." Mira backed up, releasing Sav and she dropped to her feet grinning at my sister.

"It's okay. I would have told him what happened, but your brother never listens to anyone."

"I'm so mad at him. I hope you didn't agree. I love you—of course—but he doesn't deserve you."

Sav's gaze slid to me. "You didn't tell her the truth either?"

I leaned against a wall. "And what is the truth?"

"You used me."

"Maybe I meant it."

Sav rolled her eyes. "I honestly thought so for entirely too long. What I wouldn't give to have your cold unfeeling heart."

The words were three quick jabs to my chest in rapid succession. Cold. Unfeeling. Heart. I thought I heard bone crunch on the last word. Little did she know, I'd give more than she ever would for that.

Sav crossed her arms over her chest. "So I'm the bad guy and you get to waltz in, claiming you tried your best."

"Will you forgive me?" I put as little feeling into the words as I could muster, praying to Oceanus she didn't hear how desperate I was.

Her eyes softened and I exhaled a breath I hadn't known I was holding.

"Yes. Yes of course."

I should have let her believe the lie. Let her go.

But when it came to Sav, I was the most selfish male alive. I'd raze my kingdom, start wars, make enemies of all of Faerie, just to keep her near, and that terrified me.

"Are you going back to the palace this week?" Mira stared at Sav expectantly, oblivious to my pain.

Sav smiled, the corners of her eyes crinkling as she tucked a wet strand of hair behind her ear and winced.

"What happened to your eye?" I pushed off the wall, crowding closer.

She untucked the hair from behind her ear, looking away, covering the network of tiny veins criss crossing the white of her right eye, but she was too late to hide the truth from me. I touched her cheek, brushing the strands aside and inhaled a shallow breath. It had been brutal—a black eye—but it was healing, slowly. The chill in my veins crept up my chest as icy calm took hold of me.

"The autumn prince," Sav whispered.

"The dead autumn prince?" My spies had reported his death, but none had confirmed the killer. All they knew was that he'd been burned...

I searched Sav's face. She hadn't said it outright, but her silence told me more than words ever could.

"You killed him." It was good she had. I would have reveled in watching him die slowly if he still drew breath.

Sav bit her lip, glancing between me and Mira. "I can't tell you."

Her words struck harder than any physical blow. Not just because she was hiding something, but because I knew why. I'd used her.

And this... this was the consequence.

I wrapped my fingers around hers. Damn my selfish heart, but I wasn't ready to lose her yet. "Sav. You must know, I would never use anything you told me against you. Even to aid my court."

Mira stared at me, her gaze burning the side of my face, but I ignored her.

Sav nodded slowly, looking down at our interlaced fingers. For once, she didn't pull away.

My heart soared, praying to Oceanus I hadn't lost her trust. The ice was receding, some of my frozen heart thawing at the knowledge of his death. At knowing she'd exacted revenge on the male who did that to her.

"Let's sit." Squeezing her fingers, I tugged her to a bed of seaweed, forming the strands into a settee and sat beside her.

Mira crossed the room, sitting cross legged on the floor and laid a hand on Sav's knee. "Tell us."

Sav recounted the events of her night, beginning with my dramatic exit. Mira sat in rapt silence, rare for her, until Sav mentioned Foxglove scooping Primrose up to carry her away. "Of course he did, that sexy male. What a gentle fae."

I would have scolded her, but my gut was twisting. I hadn't known about the betrothal. Primrose had used me. But I'd used her first. Used her to keep close to Sav. And now she might have paid the price.

No one truly believed Prince Helenium had waited all these centuries for a mate. He'd killed dozens of lovers—none survived more than a few nights in his bed. What was her cousin thinking, arranging such a marriage? Had he meant to send her to her death?

I bit down hard on my molars each time Sav mentioned Prince Fero. She made him out to be a hero when it was clear from her story, the male had used the incident to end a rival. Now he had Alder under his thumb and the future princess's sister was even more in his debt. He was becoming a problem. A powerful one I couldn't beat. In the ballroom, his magic wrapped around mine, I felt it. In a fight, he would win.

But a fae's power grew until they were two centuries old. He had more than one hundred and fifty years on me. One day, we would be equals and then I'd love to see who came out on top.

"And now Alder has moved the wedding up. He will marry Sage in two weeks."

I shifted in my seat. "I had two goals today." Sav watched me, waiting for the rest. "To mend things with Spring. As you know." I dipped my chin in a show of respect for her part in my deception. "And to bring you what I left to find the night everything happened." I reached into my pocket, pulling out the small pouch. "Take this each month, at the crescent moon. It will suppress your magic until your birthday. It will keep you safe from those who would be threatened by your gift."

Sav opened her palm and I set the bag down. She stared at it. "Do I eat it?"

"It's tea. You brew it."

She frowned. "I might have died that night without my gift."

"The princes are gone, your sister's wedding is on the horizon. Your only concern now is the discovery of your magic." I wrapped my fingers around hers, squeezing. "Sav I know you trust your sister, but—"

"But nothing. My sister and I are all we have. She would not harm me if she learned the truth."

I swallowed my next words. Nothing would change her mind. "Maybe you're right."

"I am."

I wasn't prepared to tell her the truth of Fero's gift. Of what I suspected he wanted from her. It would only frighten her more and if I gave away his secret, I would lose what leverage I had. I raised a hand. "But please trust me. The court is full of snakes, all of them searching for secrets to exploit. The fewer secrets you have, the better your odds of avoiding their games."

When I'd returned Sav to her home, I moved quickly over land to the lakeshore. I'd kept Sav long enough that Sage should have taken her message to Alder, but there was no telling if he would have given word to his soldiers yet. I wasn't in the mood to be struck by one of their poisoned arrows.

In my castle, I spun a silver tube on my desk, debating the merits of inciting another outburst from Sav to encourage her use of the tea. Mira stepped through the air bubble into my study and cleared her throat.

I looked up, letting the tube fall to the stone table. "Yes."

"I want to return to the spring court for the wedding."

"No."

She rounded the table, bracing a hand against it as I tipped back in my chair and watched her. She was weighing her options for this argument, but in my study—away from courtiers and spies—her screaming, her tears, none of it would sway me. Here, she had no ground.

"I know you love her."

The legs of my chair slammed to the floor. My heart hammered in my chest, each beat a blow against my ribs. I fixed my gaze on the glass floor, fighting the flood of emotion her words unleashed. Relief at being seen. Terror at what it meant. Fury that my sister could read me so easily when no one else ever had.

I stood, pacing away from Mira. I could deny it, but my heavy heart ached to share this truth with someone. I lifted a hand to the bookcase lining the wall and ran the pad of my finger over the smooth stone. My gaze trailed the rows of letters arranged neatly down each spine and the words blurred. Even now, when I was discovered, admitting it was akin to extracting my inner organs and laying them on the table for dissection. Years of hiding my truths, keeping them locked away, had made it impossible to speak the words aloud now.

I looked up, meeting Mira's inky eyes and nodded.

"But how?" She twisted her fingers together and I realized Mira didn't want my truth; she was searching for a way to use this information to her advantage. Could I blame her? She was raised in the same cold, calculating court I was. She may feel things more keenly than the others at court, but like me, she'd learned that it was only good for one thing. Leverage.

I had a moment of regret for letting my emotion lose this battle before I gave in to the crushing relief that overwhelmed everything else, and gave Mira what she wanted.

"I don't know."

"But... then you must understand how I'm suffering."

I swallowed, searching my sister's face. "And you believe what you feel for the Hawthorn prince is *love*?"

Mira's fingers tightened around each other until they were dark blue at the tips. "I know I haven't known him long, but there's a tug in my chest every time he's near and when we danced, I felt light as air." She untwisted her fingers, pushing off the desk. "I'm desperate to see him."

I glanced up from the row of books collected over nearly a decade. All the books Sav had borrowed or bargained for over the years. These were new editions, in perfect condition. One day they would be hers. For now, I was content to sit with them in my underwater palace.

"What do you know about him?"

Mira's brow furrowed. "I know he's handsome and tall—"

"I didn't ask what he looks like. Tell me something about him. Something that speaks to his character."

Her lip trembled, but then her chin lifted. "He's better than some common fae from the village. He's a prince."

My teeth ground together. I turned, stalking toward her. Her eyes widened and she stumbled back until her shoulders struck stone.

"You are no princess, Mira." Her eyes misted, and she pressed herself flat to the wall. "The title I granted you can be taken away just as easily." I stopped close enough to feel her breath quicken. "Tell me, what makes you think a prince would want you?"

Mira burst into tears, shoving past me and out of my study. She pushed through the air bubble, shifting into kelpie form and disappeared down the dark corridor.

I rubbed a hand over my face exhaling a long breath. I hadn't thought my bruised heart had room for any more cuts, but I felt Mira's anguish more deeply than she would ever know. My chest ached. My words had been cruel—cut from the same sharp knife my mother once used on me. I had hated her for that coldness, that distance. Now I saw the truth. I wasn't better than her. I was becoming her.

CHAPTER 20

Sav

The door to our small cottage slammed and I winced, looking up as my twin stormed in. "You've done it. You've ruined my life."

I bit the inside of my cheek. One sharp word and I'd lose the last scrap of control I had left. I was tired, my face hurt, and it had taken me the better part of an hour to put my books back on the shelf in their correct order. I wanted to escape to the forest. To find a tall tree to climb and sit with my thoughts until the pounding in my head stopped.

"Because of *you*," she hissed, "the alliance is falling apart. You couldn't keep your mouth shut for *one* evening, and now Alder thinks there's no reason to move the wedding forward."

I spun to face my sister. "Right. Because going to war with our oldest ally sounds like a *great* idea."

Sage's cheeks flamed and her hand flew to her hip. I mirrored her action, raising a brow.

When the silence stretched too long for Sage's comfort, she spat out: "Of course not."

I said nothing, waiting for the apology I knew would never come.

116

She huffed out a loud sigh and stormed past me slamming the door to our room. I heard the click of the mechanical lock, the one used until children were old enough to seal doors with magic. Great. Now I was locked out of *our* room.

A loud crash followed by Sage's slurred curses made my lips inch up. Until I remembered Sage never took her anger out on *her* things. "Sage! Don't you dare break my bow and arrows!"

"Ladies of court don't hunt," she shouted back.

I held my hand over my lips to keep the scream in and whirled toward the front door. I couldn't be in the house with her when she was like this. Heat crackled in my veins and a sliver of fear shot down my spine. I wasn't furious, just annoyed. But even that was enough to make the heat rise in my blood. Lately, my magic didn't wait for rage. It only needed a spark.

I flung the door open, marching into the woods behind our cottage. We were far enough from the village and the castle that no one came through our forest. It was untouched by high fae. Tugging at the laces of my stays, I inhaled a great heaving breath as I broke into a run.

Wind slapped my face, tangling in my thick hair. I tore the leather tie free and laughed as strands streamed behind me like fire. I picked up speed, each step more weightless until I could have sworn I was carried on a breeze.

The forest blurred by, creatures eyeing me as I ran. I let out a shriek, my chest lighter than it had been in weeks. This. This was what I loved. Nature. The hum of magic in every root and leaf, thrumming beneath my skin like a second heartbeat. The buzz of tiny tinks and soft hooting of crawlin in their perches. This was what Faerie was meant to be. Not castles and corsets and finery.

And I would soon be giving it up to move into the cage Sage's betrothal had bought us.

I slid to a halt glancing around. Without realizing, I'd run all the way to the border of Summer. SnapDragons hissed and gnashed their teeth, warning me to stay on my side of the line. I peered into the distance.

Although the majority of Summer was arid and barren, a portion was thickly forested, making it impossible to see beyond the border into their domain.

The memory of my one and only trip to their palace floated to my mind. To the very naked prince who had caught me spying. It was so different from Spring. So free.

"What are you doing out here?"

I spun around, heart climbing into my throat. The creature who eyed me was new, I was sure I'd never met her before, but I knew of the satyrs. They were a secretive tribe who chose not to abide by the rules of high fae and made their home across borders. Though I'd never met this satyr, I could tell by the length of her horns that she was a leader of one of the clans.

"Hello. I'm Sav."

"Fire fae." Her tone was flat, and my stomach dropped.

How could she know that? What else did she see when she looked at me?

"I will have that gift. When I turn twenty-five."

The golden-eyed satyr shook her head. "I don't think so."

My heart drummed in my chest, making it painful to breathe. "I don't know what you mean."

"Yours is not a singular gift, fire fae. You are something else."

My throat was dry, my tongue sticky against the roof of my mouth as I tried to think of some response, but the satyr didn't wait for my reply. She turned, hopping over the line between Spring and Summer and disappeared between the trees. I stared after her, lost in a spiral of thoughts, each more terrifying than the next.

Crunching leaves behind me broke my trance and I whirled around. A fox watched me from the shadows, black-eared and sharp-eyed. Its gaze held mine for a heartbeat. Its eyes matched my own. Then it vanished, as silently as it came.

CHAPTER 21

Kaspar

I straightened my cuffs, shoulders stiffening as I gave my appearance a once over. I'd stayed away for over a month. Long enough to make it look intentional. Long enough to make her think I didn't care. That hurt more than I wanted to admit, but if I didn't create distance now, they'd see it. They'd use her against me.

Autumn would announce their new ruler today. I was expected to make an appearance; to show my support. Although I wasn't a member of the land courts, I—and my uncle—had good reason to maintain a relationship with Autumn. It was, after all, the source of all natural land magic in Faerie.

"I'm coming."

I looked up at Mira's reflection in the mirror. "You're not."

"You can't keep me trapped down here forever."

"You're water fae. This is your home."

Mira stomped her foot on the floor. "My mother is land fae."

My eyes widened as my gaze shot to the open hall behind Mira. "Don't speak those words aloud. Ever."

She lowered her gaze, looking chastised for once.

I turned to face her. "Mira. You know it isn't safe for you to spend so much time on land. Least of all in a court I have no alliance with. I have no cause to bring my emissary there."

"Let me go to Spring then. To be with Sav. You must be worried about her."

I exhaled through my nose. "If I let you go—"

A shrill scream erupted from her as her face split in a wide grin.

I frowned. "If I let you go... You will not see the prince. You will stay with Sav—"

"Yes. Yes. I promise. I'm completely over him."

I tugged harder on my cuff and she shut her mouth, motioning for me to continue.

"You will not cause a scene."

She nodded.

"You will not give our courts reason to go to war."

Her cheeks darkened.

"You will not flirt with males."

Her solemn expression would have made me laugh if I didn't already think I was making a terrible mistake by even considering it. Mira never understood that a careless flirtation or a loud laugh could be interpreted as provocation. That a prince's glance or a noble's glare could mean war. She never felt the weight of a court's fury. Because I carried it for her.

"I swear. I actually find females far superior. And princes. Gross. Who needs them? They are full of themselves."

A snort escaped me.

"Except you. You're the most perfect, amazing prince—brother—who ever lived."

A smirk tugged at the corner of my lips as I marched past her, parting the water in the hall to keep my suit dry. "Come on, then."

She squealed and darted after me. "You won't regret it. I swear. I'll look after Sav and be on my best behavior and keep the peace between our courts."

"Sire."

I froze, turning to face the captain of my guard. "What is it, Acalo?"
"Sharks."

My blood ran cold. Sharks only meant one thing. Aegon. But they weren't the threat. They were the distraction. Aegon never arrived without calculating the effect of his entrance. My instinct screamed at me to act, but I couldn't afford to misstep. Not with Mira here.

I turned to warn Mira, but I was already too late. The door at the end of the hall swung open and icy, salt water rushed in, flooding the hall. I shifted quickly, changing into my kelpie form and Mira did the same. Pondweed wilted along the corridor, sea water choking every fragile bloom in its path.

I flung up a defensive shield, thwarting my uncle's plan to flood the castle by trapping his salty water in the hall. While many of the folk in my court could survive either, the creatures could not.

Two massive bull sharks charged me. I held my ground, bearing two rows of teeth at them. They halted less than a foot from my face, black eyes narrowed menacingly on me. I gave the current a shove, knocking them back and growling, stomping a hoof on the floor.

"There will be no need for that, Nephew."

The pair of sharks slid apart, clearing a path for Aegon, Prince of Oceans and Seas.

"You dare bring salt water into my castle?"

Black eyes, as depthless as the sea he commanded, trailed over my kelpie form. Where I was bright, sparkling turquoise with scales that refracted the light like shimmering glass at the bottom of a lake, he was inky darkness, a purple so murky it was nearly as black as the deepest abyss.

He smiled, black teeth on display and I bared mine in response. "I mean no offense, Nephew."

My hoof scraped the ground as he neared, causing him to halt. "You have ten seconds to declare your intentions."

My guards crowded the wall of freshwater I'd erected, waiting for my command. Aslik and Dagon, my uncle's personal guard and most trusted shark spies, circled Aegon, snapping their teeth at the gathering crowd. He had been smart bringing these two. They could survive in freshwater should I choose to push my uncle's magic back.

"I am here on a mission of peace." As if to prove his words true, he shifted into mer form. Though the scales covering his skin were still a great protection to him, he was much more vulnerable in this state and I relaxed slightly. Truly, if he'd meant war, he would have come with more than two soldiers.

I shifted in a show of good faith. "After seventeen years, you seek peace?"

Aegon raised his arms in a placating gesture. "A truce might be the more accurate description."

I ground my teeth.

"We both seek an alliance with Autumn. Let us show a united front. What better way to ensure their new ruler sees value in alliance?"

I snorted, glancing to Alaco and gave him the slightest dip of my chin to let him know my uncle could be trusted. Today. My uncle thought me a fool. Truly, did he believe me so naive? I was young for a ruler, but I had learned many years ago that being in a position of power meant watching your back at every turn.

The reminder of my one trustworthy friend, the one I'd let go to keep her safe, stung as I faced the fae who should have been the one I could rely on.

"Together then, Uncle."

I waved a hand, ushering him toward the door he'd just come through.

Mira remained frozen and I thanked Oceanus she hadn't drawn attention to herself. Perhaps she was finally learning how dangerous her position was.

CHAPTER 22

Sav

I stood, running a finger along the gold tip of my ear. The cuffs were gaudy things, and I hated them. Another shackle tying me to this castle. It had been over a month since I was allowed to leave the grounds. I could travel the maze, admire the tulips, stand at the edge of the manicured lawn and stare longingly into the forest. But I could go no farther.

"Lady Briar, Prince Hawthorn has requested your presence."

I sighed, turning. "Thank you, Rosemary." The fawn dipped low and I grimaced. I would never get used to anyone bowing and scraping for me. It was unnatural for any creature to be considered better than another. "Please. Don't."

The fawn's cheeks turned a dark shade of green, reminding me of one of the many differences between us. Like the water folk, they had a different color blood. I wasn't sure why when we were all of Faerie, but the history of our kind was shrouded in mystery. Some said Mab had traveled here, making a place for our kind among the natives. Others said nothing existed here before she dreamed it into reality.

Four portals to another realm called Earth existed, but only nobility with Mab's blessing were allowed to travel there. Those who did brought back strange tales, saying the creatures there resembled high fae and Mab more than any of us.

I had never dreamed of leaving Faerie, but perhaps, if Mab granted me permission, I could escape this realm and find freedom in another.

I moved swiftly down the hall to the throne room. Rosemary rushed ahead to open the door. I frowned and reached for the handle, but her gaze darted to the floor as she pulled it wide, leaving me standing at the entrance with dozens of courtiers staring at me.

I cleared my throat, and stepped inside, marching down the long aisle. Eyes tracked me, cataloging every imperfection. Just a villager in borrowed silks. A girl playing dress-up. I held my head high. The folk of my village were worth ten times what these courtiers were.

"Sav Briar." Alder stared down his nose at me, the throne beside him empty as my sister had yet to say her vows. "You rejected a match that would have meant peace between Spring and Lakes and Streams."

Hisses erupted in the crowd, and I felt their hateful glares on my back. I pushed my shoulders back. I had known this would come. Whether Kaspar intended to place me in this position or not, I did not fault him for using me to stop a war between our two courts. It was a small price for peace.

"But," Alder said and the room quieted. "You can be of value to your prince yet."

My stomach soured as my mind raced over the myriad of ways he might punish me. It would be futile to point out that Mab would very likely reject the union. I had wronged my prince and I would pay.

"You will be our emissary in the summer court."

Ice sliced down my spine and it was an effort to hold myself upright at his proclamation. Summer was not our ally. They had not come to any terms with Spring. Blood drained from my face and I swayed on my feet. I never imagined it would come to this. He was sending me to my death wearing a silk ribbon and calling it diplomacy.

"Brother." Foxglove, the younger Hawthorn prince, spoke from the crowd, but his words were faint against the pounding of my heart. Alder didn't know, couldn't know, the power Prince Fero held over me. But he did know what his proclamation meant.

Foxglove was still speaking, but blood was pulsing in my ears and heat boiled my veins. Distantly, I remembered the tea. Why hadn't I taken the tea? I was burning up from the inside and my magic was desperate for release. The tea would have saved me.

Long fingers wrapped around my arm and Foxglove's bright eyes darted to my bare skin. It must have been scalding to the touch, but he said nothing, grip loosening only a fraction. I gasped, hands twitching with the urge to ignite. The fire clawed, begging to be unleashed.

"Lord Banyan will make a fine match. And his lands, situated near Autumn's border, will give us the advantage we need to form better alliances with their new ruler."

The words circled my mind, trying to gain purchase in my head. I breathed in and out through my nose. What was he saying? What was he promising on my behalf?

Alder clapped his hands together, startling me out of my panicked haze. All at once, the room came into focus, the sounds and smells too sharp for my senses. I wasn't yet twenty-five. Why was everything so sharp?

"What do you say, Lady Briar?"

I glanced up at Foxglove, noting the way his fingers only hovered over my skin now. "Say to what?"

He gave a polite chuckle and the room tittered with laughter at my expense. "Will you allow our eligible Lord Banyan to court you?"

A male stepped forward and held out his hand. I sucked in a breath and looked to Lord Hawthorn, hoping I would find a friend in the prince. He felt the heat scorching under his palms and must have guessed my secret, but had said nothing in front of the court and his sovereign. Would he force me to reveal it now?

Lord Banyan's hand was still outstretched and my gaze dipped to it, terror roiling in my gut. The tea would've spared me this. Would've kept the fire buried.

"Allow me to escort Lady Briar to the evening's ball, Lord Banyan. She's eager to meet you in the ballroom."

A muscle in the lord's jaw jumped and I tracked the movement. My pulse steadied. Not calm—but no longer hammering. *Court you.* The words sprang to the forefront of my mind. This was a suitor. A lord. From my own court. An eligible prospect rather than a power move by my family. My heart rate slowed and my gaze met his. He wasn't classically handsome, or as tall as the male I'd once imagined beside me.

But there was an earnestness in his gaze that set me at ease.

The heat in my veins was cooling, and I accepted Foxglove's out-stretched hand, allowing him to lead me from the room. My heart was returning to its normal rhythm, my breathing slowing. His grip held me steady as we moved past the room of jeering onlookers. I felt Alder's assessing gaze on my back and could only thank Mab that Sage hadn't been here to witness my first official appearance in court. She would be so disappointed in me.

In the ballroom, instead of releasing me to melt into the shadows as I'd seen him do so many times before, Foxglove led me into the first dance of the evening. Several others from court joined in and Lord Banyan stood beside the dancefloor, tracking our movement.

"How is Mira?"

His words startled me and my gaze swung from the onlookers back to him. He was impossibly tall and I stretched my head back to look up at him.

"I have not spoken to the emissary of Lakes and Streams of late."

It was only a half lie. She'd visited me twice, without her brother's knowledge I was sure, and we had regrouped after the not proposal, but apart from that, she, and the other folk of Lakes and Streams, had been absent from my life.

I knew things would change when we left our small cottage. I had expected it. A prince couldn't simply sneak in at night when father was asleep. This was a castle, with guards and protocols. One must be announced, make an appointment. Still, his absence left a cold ache in its wake.

His brow dipped and something like true remorse shone on his face.

"She does not blame you."

Foxglove's grip tightened on mine, a small smile threatening to break on his face. Perhaps I had misjudged the prince. He was a Hawthorn, but Prim was of their bloodline and she had proved to be an invaluable friend. I would not have survived at court this month without her steady presence.

Since the incident with Prince Helenium, something had changed in my friend. Her daring spirit had been muted. When I'd last visited her rooms, her dark walls were replaced by soft pastels. It was a small change, but it meant a great deal.

"I can pass her a message."

Amethyst eyes met mine and they burned with some emotion I couldn't name. Foxglove hadn't lived at the palace with his brother as a child. He was the son of their father's mistress. The woman he'd been rumored to love even before he's been forced to wed a woman with earth magic.

Although he was born nearly two centuries before me, folk still talked of the great injustice done to the prince's mistress. She was his mate. The one he should have married, but the rules in Spring were clear. A Hawthorn heir must marry the most powerful earth fae in our court. Mating played no part in it. When she took her vows, joined the family, her magic fed the land.

Sage claimed hers was a love match, but I had yet to see Alder show her the kind of affection she desired. The kind our father had shown mother. Perhaps being raised outside the palace walls had made Foxglove different from the other fae at court.

"It is for the best that we parted when we did."

Foxglove's stilted words and sweaty palms only endeared him to me. That he'd taken an interest in Mira, someone the high fae, especially the royals, would consider beneath them, made me reconsider what lay beneath the stoic facade he presented to the world.

The doors to the ballroom swung wide, slamming against two of Creig's soldiers stationed beside the wall. They grunted, recovering quickly as all eyes traveled to the door.

Mira stepped through, a glittering dress falling off her shoulders and spilling to the floor. Unlike the short dresses she'd worn before, this one trailed her, refracting fae light off every surface. If her dramatic entrance hadn't caught our attention, her glittering gown would have.

Foxglove stopped, halting me with him.

Mira cleared her throat, looking around the room sheepishly. Eyes landing on me, she broke into a wide grin and strode confidently through revelers who parted as she made her way to the dancefloor.

I watched her approach, but her gaze slid from me to my dance partner. Foxglove's hand left my back as he stepped around me, straining to reach her. They collided in a tangle of limbs, rushing into the next dance.

Cheeks flushing, I left the dancefloor, hoping no one had noticed my hasty departure. Mira had a way of turning discomfort into spectacle. Even her entrance looked intentional. Mine had been quiet—forgettable.

"May I?"

I turned, finding Lord Banyan in a similar position to the one I'd met him in in the throne room. This time, I took his hand, grateful that I hadn't just become the social pariah of the evening. He wrapped an arm around my back, leading me onto the dance floor. My gaze traveling back to Mira and Foxglove. She draped her arms over his shoulders leaning close, his face hidden in the sweep of her hair, whispering in her ear.

Their unabashed interest in one another made my heart swell. I longed to be that free with someone. To openly show my affection and have it returned. I glanced at my partner, finding his eyes on me and gave him a small smile. Could I have that with this male?

He searched my face, but I felt none of the joy I'd seen in Mira. Instead, an insidious feeling crawled across my skin. As though he were cataloguing my every fault to store for later. "You truly are a replica of the future princess, aren't you?"

My throat dried and my hands grew clammy. We'd been compared before. Twins were rare among the high fae. But *future princess*? That sank like a stone. I hadn't thought how valuable my face might be to someone chasing a crown.

I laughed nervously, attempting to pull out of his grip. His hand tightened around my fingers. "Where do you think you're going?"

I swallowed. Searching his face for any of the kindness I'd seen before.

"You will not embarrass me. At least your sister understands what's expected of a common fae elevated to such a rank."

I frowned. Heat surged again, angrier this time. Closer to the surface. Lord Banyan's eyes widened as he loosened his hold on me. I tried to tamp it down, to stop the flames I knew were coming. It had been a near thing in the throne room. This time, I wouldn't be able to control it.

Lord Banyan hissed, releasing me. "Bitch."

The room was spinning, the music impossibly loud and I pressed my hands to my temples to drown it out. Fire burned in my chest, scorching me from the inside and I was helpless to stop it. I would reveal my secret to everyone here. Why couldn't I control it? What was wrong with me? No other fae had this affliction.

Burning fingers wrapped around mine, tugging my hands down and the fire in my veins receded. The blaring music in my ears dulled to a melodic rhythm and my heart slowed. I blinked up into orange eyes. Flames danced in his irises and the temperature in my own body cooled. Slowly, the magic drained from me. I gasped with the weight of it removed.

Prince Fero nodded, saying nothing as he led me into a dance. One arm wrapped around me, hand cupping mine, my step lightened and for the first time in months, the oppressive weight of the magic coursing through my veins abated.

We spun, moving with the music and thankfully, my hands weren't burning or clammy. I felt normal. As I had for twenty four years. "What's wrong with me?" I whispered.

"Nothing." Prince Fero's eyes burned with unchecked fury and I shrank under the weight of his stare. He swallowed down his rage, spinning us faster. We circled past Lord Banyan who was glaring at us both. "Don't marry him."

I grimaced. "Spoken like a true prince." The anger was back in his eyes, but where he touched me, my skin was almost cool. Although his was a furnace, it didn't burn me. "Why doesn't it hurt?"

He knew what I meant. "Fire fae cannot burn one another."

I turned the words over in my mind. Had I known that? Had anyone told me?

"And," he said. I looked up. Into his eyes. "It's your magic in my veins."

I faltered, losing my footing. "What?" Was this his true innate gift? I'd believed he was a magic sensor, but was he something more? Could he steal magic?

"Should I buy you a lexicon? You seem to have a limited vocabulary."

I snorted a laugh, tugging my hand from his to cover my mouth.

"Don't pretend with me, Lady. Your very good friend has chosen to use it against me after all."

I frowned, brows furrowing.

Prince Fero's grip loosened, his arm going slack at my back. "You didn't know? I thought..."

I waited as we continued to spin.

"I thought you told him after you burned away my compulsion the night we met."

I bit down on my tongue before I could say *what* again. Every time we spoke I had more questions than answers. My head began to spin. Thankfully, the magic didn't rise up to consume me.

He watched me as I puzzled over his words. I glanced around the room. Mira still danced with Foxglove; Lord Banyan had thankfully left and Sage... Sage was glaring daggers at her fiancé while he ran his tongue up the side of another female's neck. I halted.

The prince lifted me off my feet, spinning me easily. I tried to tug my hand from his grip, but he held tighter. "Don't interfere in their business," he said quietly, too close to my ear. "Not here."

I glared up at him struggling in his hold. "That's my sister. Put me down!"

He stiffened, setting me down and I backed up, glancing around at the eyes on us. That fury was back in the prince's eyes, but I didn't have time to waste on him or his confusing words. I rushed to Sage's side, wrapping an arm around her shoulder. "Sage, come. Let's get a drink."

She dug her nails into my arm but let me lead her away from the male she would marry in a month. Rage boiled in my gut, but I shut the feeling down, terrified of burning my sister. Her rage would have to be enough for us both.

CHAPTER 23

Kaspar

The autumn palace was just as my father had described it. An ancient fortress older than all the rest. Magic thrummed through it. Not a castle built, but buried. I'd never visited Winter, but I had a feeling even their palace wasn't as old or wild as this one. Where each of the other courts had built their castles to command the space—to dominate it—Autumn's castle was carved from the sheerest cliff face. It was made for defense.

Trolls, strongest of the low fae, were said to have carved Autumn's palace long before Mab arrived. Deep in the caves, they still mined gems. But some whispered they harvested something older. Wilder.

These were the legends sea folk never shared with the high fae.

Now that I was here, staring up at the wall of white stone, magic buzzed under my skin, swirling through me. It begged me to connect with it. I wondered briefly how Sav's magic would have reacted.

Aegon stopped beside me, slapping me on the back. Water splashed my cheek and I shrugged out of his touch, dipping back below the stream we'd traveled to get here. Unlike me, my uncle wasn't blessed with Luna's shifting magic. He could only hold two forms. While only those sea fae with the gift of shifter magic were blessed with the ability to walk on land when they chose, I was unique in that I was as comfortable on land as I was in water. I—and Mira.

I suspected her ability derived from having a land parent. But I had no such parent. My thoughts circled back to my father. Had he kept a secret from us? The thought should've unsettled me. Instead, it drifted away like silt on a current.

We traveled upstream, Aslik and Dagon at our backs. My guard traveled several paces behind, boxing my uncle in. If he was concerned with their presence, or with being trapped in my stream with no easy escape, he showed none of it. Either he was not as cautious as I'd always thought him to be, or he knew something I didn't. My cold blood chilled. I didn't like it.

Swimming under the waterfall bisecting our path, I felt the wards working to repel all those who were not invited and glanced back at the sharks, and my guard-, forced to wait on the other side. I nodded to Alaco and he spun around, retreating. He would wait at Spring's border unless I gave the signal.

Autumn was the only court surrounded on all sides by land. That made attack by sea impossible without my aid. I had known my uncle's true purpose in coming together was to warn Autumn that none were safe from his reach.

I shifted, stepping out of the stream and onto land.

The outfit I'd laid out in my office reappeared and I straightened my cuffs once more, the itchy fabric of the shirt I was forced to wear for the occasion, irritating against my skin.

"Kaspar."

I glanced back at my uncle's darkening face, swallowing the smile tugging at my lips. "Shall I meet you inside Uncle?"

Purple brows slashed low on his forehead and he scowled before ducking below the water once more, following its path into the lower mines.

I stepped closer to the wall, wrapping an arm around a thick vine and let it pull me up. I reached the entrance, stepping through massive doors swung wide to receive visitors, and magicked the dust from my suit, glancing around the cavernous space lit only by low fae light.

Trolls were said to hate light, but I had expected the high fae residing here to be less concerned with the needs of their low folk. Unlike Spring, who forced their low fae into positions of servitude and labor, it seemed this court may be different.

"Prince Kaspar! Welcome!"

I looked up and up at the gargantuan troll who had melted from the wall to greet me. I blinked, looking him over. Although I knew there were different kinds of trolls, I'd yet to see a rock troll in the flesh. Stories of their strength and brutality in battle were legendary among my kind and, as a child, I'd listened in fascination as the soldiers of my court told of the warriors who nearly destroyed Spring in the great battle.

"I am honored." I tilted my head to the side. A show of respect but not deference.

The large stone creature let out a deep gravelly chortle and ushered me to follow. Heavy steps scraped over the uneven floor as he lumbered at a snail's pace. He led me down a long hall lined on either side with intricate carvings depicting battles the warriors here must have fought over the centuries.

No one knew how old Mab was, thousands of years at least, but as we traveled deeper into the castle, the carvings grew more rudimentary and faint and I wondered again just how old the autumn court was. Had the trolls once ruled the land as father said kelpies had ruled the sea? Had we, by some twist of fate, been spared domination by virtue of living under water alone?

In the near dark, my eyes adjusted slowly, but the sound of running water filled my ears, ions buzzing through the air to lend my senses strength, and soon I could make out the shapes around me. It was a massive room stretching far into the recesses of this fortress and all around me, creatures lined the walls, still as statues.

Heels clacked loudly over stone and a fair-haired female with blood red eyes and porcelain skin appeared from the depths. She rushed forward, kissing both my cheeks and I held in my grimace, remembering too late it was the custom in their court. "We are so pleased to have you, Prince Kaspar of Lakes and Streams." She glanced over my shoulder. "Have you come alone? We were informed your uncle would be with you as well."

Her thickly accented Elvish was strange against my ears. Another reminder that this court chose to distance themselves from the others. The high fae here were fluent in Druinin, the language of the trolls, and by the heaviness of her accent, it seemed they often defaulted to the trolls native language rather than forcing them to adopt Elvish as was expected in other courts.

My own kind's language had been lost to history. Few even remembered basic words. Envy colored my mood.

"He is just below in the mines."

The female nodded. "I'm Dahlia. I will be your host this evening. May I show you to a room before the festivities begin?"

I nodded and she led me through the large space to another long hall. This one wound and narrowed with several connecting passages breaking off from it. While nothing like the spring court in appearance, the twisting maze-like layout was familiar. I would have dearly loved to bring one of my spies. Their time would have been well spent exploring the hidden treasures of this castle.

Dahlia's deep red gown shimmered unnaturally in the low light, casting the hall in a ruby hue and magic seemed to waft from it, lulling my senses into one of calm acceptance. My interest in exploring waned the longer she remained by my side even though I fought the magic's pull. I couldn't tell if it was coming from my host or her gown, though.

The thought made me smile. A gown with magic of its own? My senses must be muddled.

In my room, the light flickered as though the magic pulsed through the very room and I shook myself to stop from staring into its hypnotic flame. *Get a hold of yourself, Kaspar.* I tugged at the water clinging to my skin in the damp place and chilled it, splashing it across my face. It did little to revive my senses as though even the water in this place was laced with the strange magic.

I spared a moment's thought for my uncle. They would have offered him rooms on the lowest level of the castle. Ones where my streams bisected the space and water moved freely. It was strange thinking of how much of my water flowed through this castle and yet I'd never spent time here.

Even as I had the thought it slipped from my mind, sliding away like a memory that wanted to be forgotten.

A knock sounded at the door, rousing me from a daze. I had no idea how long I'd been staring at the flames on the adjacent wall, but I strained to pull my gaze from the light, Dahlia beckoning me toward her, scarlet lips split in a wide inviting grin.

My feet floated after her, as if caught in a current. I reached out—her hair slipped through my fingers like water.

Dahlia turned, sparkling eyes alighting in amusement. "My magic doesn't usually work so well on your kind, Prince."

Through the haze, ice slid down my spine. I *should* be afraid of that sentence; it meant she knew something important about me, something I didn't want her to, but I couldn't remember what.

Her grin widened, showing off sharp canines, like mine, meant for tearing flesh. My flesh? The thought sent heat spearing through my abdomen, lower. I wanted her to bite me, to taste my sweet blue blood. To feast on it. And if she did, I wasn't sure I'd stop her.

I looked down. My feet had stopped moving. We were in a room. Not the grand one we'd come through before. This was smaller. Lined in red fae light. Dahlia and I were alone. I closed the distance between us but when I tried to lift my arms, they were stuck to my sides. I glanced down, finding a massive pair of arms, carved from granite, wrapped around my middle.

Not alone. Ah well. It was for the best. Sav wouldn't approve.

"Who is Sav?"

I looked up, meeting crimson eyes. Had I said the words aloud?

"Princess."

Dahlia shook her head and laughed. "Not one that I know of."

I shook my head. Not *a* princess. *My* princess. I tried to open my mouth, to correct her, but she pressed a porcelain finger to my lips.

"Now then, Prince. Let us see what your future holds."

A flicker of light warped behind her, casting my shadow long against the stone wall. Far below, something pulsed in the rock. A heartbeat. No. Drums. Distant. Faint. As if the walls remembered a war that hadn't yet happened. Not my shadow exactly—taller, broader, crown stretching into long jagged spikes. I blinked and it was gone.

CHAPTER 24

Sav

S age slammed her empty glass down on the low table at the back of the ballroom, lifting a third to her lips. "This will not be borne."

Mira crossed her arms over her chest. "I will transform right now and trample him."

My heart picked up speed. I didn't have the luxury of hoping she was joking. Kaspar would never forgive me if war broke out in his absence. "Mira, he's the prince."

She huffed loudly. "He isn't even being discreet."

Foxglove approached. We all turned our glares on him as he smiled. "Might I suggest fresh air, ladies?"

If looks could burn, he'd have gone up in flames. He backed up, hands raised.

"Let's kill him."

My eyes went wide. I whisper-shouted, "Sage! That's treason."

Mira nodded. "I'm in."

I gaped "He's the Prince."

"You're right. I have to wait till we're married."

138

I sighed. Sage would forget this the moment he smiled at her again. Princes took lovers in every court; some princesses too, though less often. She knew it.

"You need your own distraction."

Sage brightened. "Or revenge. What do you think, his half-brother or another prince?"

"Touch him and die." Mira's voice was low, almost gentle. But her eyes had gone cold—the kind of cold only a sea fae could achieve.

Sage blinked, genuinely confused. Of course she hadn't noticed Mira and Foxglove these past weeks. She saw nothing beyond herself.

"Perhaps someone that wouldn't start a war?" I suggested.

Sage nodded. "Half brother."

Mira's arm shot out, barring her path. "No."

Sage's cheeks flushed. She darted a look at me, but I only leaned against the wall. For once, her fury wasn't aimed at me. She shoved, but Mira didn't budge.

"Get out of my way, Lowborn."

My mouth fell open. "Sage."

Mira's nostrils flared, scales rippling down her arms. "What did you say?"

"I said. Move. Horse."

Mira's eyes flashed and it was the only warning we had before she shifted, transforming into a massive navy kelpie. Her hoof struck marble as she snorted loudly and the music halted. All eyes landed on us.

I flung up my arms. "Mira! You can't challenge the future princess."

Her breath blasted cold over my face, frost biting my fingertips. Panic surged. If her secret gift showed here, she was dead.

"Mira," I pleaded. "Get your magic under control."

Ice crept across the glass, spreading fast. My pulse spiked. If anyone saw—

Heat surged through my veins. This time, instead of fearing it, I reached for it. Commanded it. The fire answered. It flooded from my core into my palms, pressing against the glass until droplets welled and slid down the pane, washing away every trace of Mira's mistake.

Sage's gasp pierced my chest, sharp as a blade. Betrayal hollowed me, and my control slipped. Fire tore from my fingertips. It leapt like it had been caged too long, desperate to escape. Flames caught the vines and raced upward, as if they already knew the path. Not merely alive—hungry. They devoured the walls, cracked across the ceiling, and dragged smoke and screams in their wake.

I stumbled back, my hand trembling. I hadn't summoned the magic, but it had answered me anyway. Frantic, I searched the hall for anyone with water magic. Mira couldn't risk revealing her gift. Kaspar wasn't here.

Sage's eyes narrowed, sharp with judgment, before she turned on her heel and stormed out. Mira's widened, then she bolted, hooves striking marble as she fled. And I was left standing in the wreckage, smoke thick around me, the weight of it pressing down.

A stream of water erupted from across the room, spraying the ceiling while more folk dashed out, escaping the scorched vines crashing to the floor. I peered through the fog, but my gaze shot up once more when fire roared and crackled, seeming to battle the wave of water attempting to wrestle it into submission.

Strong arms grabbed me around the waist, carrying me out of the ballroom and I tilted my head up, staring at the underside of the orc general's chin. "Please," I whispered. "Don't arrest me. It was an accident."

He said nothing, shoving through the crowd as he carried me outside. He set me down, spinning on his heel to race back into the smoking castle. I stared around the gardens filled with milling folk, limbs trembling. No one looked my way. Could I be that lucky? Or had they simply not realized I was the one who was responsible?

Sharp nails dug into my arm, spinning me around. Relief rushed through me when I saw my sister unharmed and in one piece. I flung my arms around her. "I was so worried I'd hurt you!" She stiffened in my arms, and I released her, leaning back to search her face. I'd never seen so much rage in her expression before. Underneath, I saw the hurt, the betrayal, and my chest ached. "Sage. I can explain."

She didn't speak. Didn't blink. For the first time in our lives, my sister looked at me like a stranger.

"Please. I didn't mean to. I can't control it."

She crossed her arms over her chest, burying her trembling fingers. "You will answer for this."

Ice sliced through me and I stumbled back. "No. Sage. You can't tell anyone. I'm not supposed to have magic yet."

Her eyes narrowed, grip tightening around her biceps. "I won't be branded a traitor with you. Keeping your secret would mean punishment for me too."

My heart slammed against my ribcage making it hard to breathe. My sister was petty, vain and sometimes selfish, but until this moment, I'd never thought her cruel. All the times Kaspar had warned me flooded back, racing through my mind.. Would she truly send her own sister to the dungeon or worse, the mines?

"I would recommend against it, Lady Briar."

My gaze swiveled left to the other Hawthorn prince and fresh panic sliced through me.

Sage turned her angry stare on Foxglove. "Threatening your future queen, Foxglove? In a matter of weeks I will outrank you."

He slid a hand in his pocket, less affected by her mood than I was. "Not at all. My brother is ill tempered at the best of times. Should you tell him your twin set fire to his ball, he would not look upon you kindly. It is far more likely he would name you her conspirator."

Sage raised her chin, staring down at her nose at the much taller male. "I'm his future queen. He wouldn't dare."

Foxglove raised a brow. "Your uncle told you of the failed match with Autumn?"

Sage went impossibly pale and I glanced between her and the prince. *Failed match? Autumn?*

He nodded. "I thought as much. Would you give him provocation to end your engagement when you are so close to getting what you most desire?"

Sage's gaze darkened but her lips remained pressed together.

My gaze tracked movement at the edge of my vision as a wave of power bowled over me, knocking me back. I staggered, glancing around, but no one else seemed to be affected. I searched the darkened hedges behind us for any sign of the prince that I knew was nearby.

"What happens the next time she does it? I can't protect her if she remains at court. Someone will see."

I turned back to Sage, my words coming out in a rush. "I have tea. Kaspar brought it to me. It will suppress my magic until I turn twenty-five." Foxglove eyed me with interest and Sage relaxed her grip on her arms. "I'll start taking it right away. Tonight. I'll go back to the cabin right now."

A sliver of pain shot through me. I'd known she'd be upset if she learned I was keeping secrets from her, but her coldness stung.

"Go." Sage spit out. "I don't want to see you at court until you have your magic under control."

I bit my lip. I longed to hug her. To apologize again for not telling her my secret, but she had erected a wall between us and only the tea, and time, would bring it down.

Turning, I ran from court, darting into the forest. I ran faster, tugging my hair free. I ran until the world was quiet again. Until I could believe, for a moment, that nothing had changed.

CHAPTER 25

Kaspar

I blinked, staring around the Hollow Wood. Scrubbing a hand over my face, I blinked again holding my hand up to the light. Faint traces of magical runes were drawn over the backs of my hands, some wrapping around my fingers and ending at the tips. I glanced down, finding more of the strange markings on my skin. In shifted form, my scales didn't cover the tender flesh on my chest and abdomen.

Diamonds in fading red ink, dots and lines, all wrapped around my middle, trailing up my sides. The marks stung faintly, like nettles beneath my skin. A metallic scent lingered, not mine. Not sea-born. I stood on shaky legs and stumbled toward the stream I sensed nearby. Calling the current for aid, I brought the water to me, letting it carry me the rest of the way.

Sinking beneath the surface, I took my true form, gaze trailing over the dissipating red magic lifting from my body.

Dahlia's bleary words came back to me. *My magic doesn't usually work so well on your kind.* She had done something to me. Something that shouldn't have worked, but I wasn't full kelpie. I couldn't be. The truth

sank into my bones even as the last of Autumn's magic bled from my skin. What had they done to me? What had I divulged?

Bits and pieces of the night fought to slip through the haze that still wrapped around my mind, muddling the memory.

A room rimmed in crimson light and stone trolls. Dahlia, chanting as she drew symbols on my flesh in blood. Not paint. Not glamour. Blood. High fae, if my instincts were right. A blood ritual—and I had no idea what I'd given away. I slapped my neck, the sting of her bite tingling. Her face, leaning back to stare at me as she wiped her hand across the back of her mouth. "What are you, Prince of Lakes and Streams?"

I shuddered, gaining strength as the current flowing through me carried me farther away from the autumn court and the secrets they held.

I reached my lake in a matter of hours, diving deep. At the bottom, I pressed my forehead to the sea glass floor, drinking in the magic that would restore my senses and revive my memories. I had to know what they had learned. Had to discover what they planned to do with the information.

"Sire."

Slowly, I lifted my head, meeting Alaco's steel grey eyes. He was a silver fish, a strong leader of his pack and my most trusted soldier. Knowing he was safe, not caught in some fae trap, loosened the tension in my chest a fraction. As memories rushed in, my uncle and his guards swam to the forefront. We were not allies, but if he was caught, trapped by the autumn court, only I could rescue him.

"My uncle?"

"He left the court days ago. We have been searching for you for more than a week. Scouring the perimeter both over land and by stream looking for a way past their troll magic."

"More than a week?" I rubbed my temple. The magic should have cleared the fog—should have removed all their magic from my system—but it seemed I was still missing days of my life. Ice shot through me.

I swam for my castle, for the room at the lowest level; the root of my family's magic. I needed something stronger to break free of the seer's hold on me. *Dahlia was a seer.* That much I did remember. Had they chosen a new prince or princess? Had there been a ceremony or had it all been a ploy to lure me in?

Shoving pondweed aside, I grimaced at the state of my castle. Repairs were needed after my uncle's visit and the lingering salt was affecting the ph. Soon members of my court would become sick. I began a mental checklist of all that would need to be done.

Reaching the stone floor at the center of the castle, I ran my tongue over the pearlescent grooves of the shell and hovered over the enormous clam. Slowly, it creaked, a long tongue rolling out and I dropped onto the spongy surface. Its tongue wrapped around me, cocooning me in its restorative magic and tucked me safely inside the shell, closing and blocking out the tainted water.

A ball of shimmering light bloomed at the clam's center, so bright it seared my vision. I shut my eyes against the blast as it shot through me, tearing Autumn's magic from my blood. It fought to stay, writhing as it was dragged free. My mind burned. My body spasmed. The autumn court did not give up its secrets willingly.

I exhaled through my gills, water clean and cold. For a moment, true calm wrapped around me.

Then the memories surged.

Dahlia's voice, soft and lethal. My uncle's demands. The seer's crimson symbols etched in high fae blood.

Where is it? What did your father do with it? Where is the magic that belongs in the heart of the sea?

I didn't know. But whatever it was, they believed I did.

The clam cracked open, releasing me into the open current. My mind churned: A hidden magic. My father's betrayal. A court alliance between land and sea. What did it all mean?

"Sire." Alaco's voice cut through the haze.

I turned toward him, only now noticing the tension in his posture.

"What is it?"

"It's Mira," he said. "She's missing."

CHAPTER 26

Sav

Several days earlier

True to her word, Sage had welcomed me back to court once she was satisfied the tea was working. I wasn't sure how hurling knives at my head had convinced her, but at least she wasn't pretending I didn't exist. For that much, I was grateful.

Yet something between us had cracked that night. Not wide enough to break us apart, but enough for the ache to settle in my chest when I looked at her. I had always believed our bond was unshakable. Now... even beside her, I felt the tear between us pulling at the seams of everything we'd been.

We were less than two weeks from Sage's wedding and my stomach erupted in butterflies every time I thought of the day. It was sibling empathy, I was sure. I had nothing to be nervous about. I wasn't the one marrying a male and ascending a throne. *My* magic wouldn't be feeding all of Spring.

Sage squeezed my hand so hard I could swear bones cracked as I walked with her up the long carpeted path. On the day, she would walk alone, I

would be at the back to show encouragement, but we practiced as one, as we had done so many other things in life.

"No. Slower. This isn't a race. Do you want the guest to think you so eager? So desperate for my crown?"

Sage's cheeks flushed crimson, but I scowled up at the vile prince, meeting his wild eyed stare with defiance. He smirked at me, but his focus quickly shifted back to my sister.

"Again. And this time walk like a grownup."

Sage yanked her hand from mine as if I'd burned her. I touched my palm to my skirt, half-expecting heat. Nothing. Just the sting Alder's words always left behind.

If a dagger found its way into his left eye I wouldn't be the slightest bit sorry.

Sage marched back down the aisle to the door and spun around, glaring daggers at her prince. If he noticed, or cared, he didn't show it.

I slid into a seat watching her slow progression. As the minutes dragged on, she only seemed to slow her step. She was being intentional at this point.

"No. No. No!"

I shook my head, leaning back in my chair. It would be a long afternoon.

"Are you excited?"

I glanced to my left as Foxglove slid into the chair beside me. "About what?" I whispered. I hadn't seen much of him since the ball that had ended so disastrously, but he'd been slowly winning me over the more I got to know him. And if Mira trusted him, perhaps I should too.

"The dinner Lord Banyan has planned for you tonight?"

I twisted my mouth into the best approximation of a smile I could muster. Although my first encounter with him had gone poorly, everyone at court spoke highly of him and my sister had threatened a permanent rift if I didn't do my part for the family. Uncle Robin stopped by to remind me the alternative was a very short life in the summer court.

I couldn't admit to any of them that I wasn't as sure as they were that Prince Fero was evil. I was nearly certain now that he had been the fae to put out the fire, and though I couldn't interpret that wave of power that had washed over me as anything other than a threat, he hadn't told anyone my secret.

Kaspar would caution me against trusting anyone at court, especially those whose agenda was unclear, but I wasn't so sure he was the evil prince everyone made him out to be.

"Can't wait."

Foxglove's auburn brow arched high on his forehead. "Do you not enjoy his attention? There are other suitable males at court."

My gaze slid to his again as Alder shouted a slew of curses at the low fae arranging centerpieces. I wasn't sure why they'd brought them in. I had always been told snipping flowers in Spring was akin to high treason. Here life was retained at all cost. Ours was the burden of growing flora to feed the realm healing magic and herbs. What did it signify? The thought reminded me of Prim. She'd been absent for weeks; on a diplomatic mission to Winter.

An impossible mission if anyone had asked me. Which they hadn't.

In the history of faerie, I had only heard of one story which involved the queen of faerie attending a wedding. Prince Firethorn, gone centuries before I was born, was Mab's only son and expected to rule one day. If she ever chose to step down. His death caused the strict rules that governed Faerie and was said to be the reason Mab no longer traveled the realm. She had never recovered from his loss.

Had he not died so tragically, we may have been free to marry and bear children between courts.

"I am perfectly happy with him." I patted Foxglove's hand, returning my attention to Sage and Alder as a table crashed to the floor and Sage jumped back, narrowly avoiding the dark liquid that would have ruined her dress.

"I cannot spend another moment in your presence." Alder stormed down the aisle, turning sharply in the hall.

All eyes swiveled to Sage and she straightened her shoulders. "Clean this up. I want it out of the carpet before you sleep tonight."

The fawn nearest her bobbed low and raced through an unseen door at the back of the throne room.

"I should console my sister."

I stood, but Foxglove grabbed my hand, causing me to turn back to face him.

"She will need to keep that fighting spirit if she has any hope of surviving my brother."

I swallowed, tugging my hand free. I didn't doubt his words and a hollow feeling settled in my stomach. Nothing I said would convince my sister to back out of this marriage and I wasn't sure she could have even if she wanted to. The Lady of the Lake had spoken and the court had accepted it. This would be Sage's life in two weeks.

A grin split my lips as Primrose slid a leg over the side of a massive wolf and dropped to the ground. "Welcome home."

She rushed forward, wrapping her arms around me. It was more affection than I'd received from my own sister, and I let her warmth envelop me longer than was proper. When she released me, stepping back, the grin that stretched across her face was infectious.

"Did you do it? Did you convince her?"

Her smile fell, but she waved a hand. "Convince Mab? It was never going to happen."

I searched her face for any sign of disappointment, but found only genuine happiness. She grabbed my hands, tugging me toward the castle, glancing over a shoulder at me. "I have so much to tell you."

I followed, squeezing her hand.

In her room she set her bag on the floor and flopped onto her bed, patting the space beside her. I dropped heavily onto the soft bedding. Hers was the softest I'd ever laid on, even compared with the finery in my new room. She rolled onto her side, propping a hand against her head.

"Winter is everything you could have imagined. The magic. The balls. The fae." Primrose's cheeks flushed pink and long auburn lashes lowered.

I sat up. "Primrose Magnolia. Do you have a lover?"

She looked up, eyes going wide and dropped her head into the blankets screaming into them. "Not *a* lover. Lovers. Two. The two most perfect folk I've ever met."

My mouth fell open and I shoved her shoulder. "Who? How?"

"They are together. They invited me to join them."

Prim's door banged open and Mira stepped through. "Did I hear you say two lovers?"

Prim's cheeks flamed and she shushed Mira. "Close the door! How did you hear me in the hall?"

Mira beamed at us both. "I was spying." The wicked glint in her eye told me this wasn't her first time doing so and I laughed. I kept nothing from Mira. My secrets were hers. But I was willing to bet she had plenty of juicy gossip to share with us.

"Mira. Air shield." Prim glanced to the door and Mira nodded, throwing up a bubble of air to block any who dared to listen in outside the door.

"Spill."

Prim sat up as Mira sank onto the bed beside us. "Well, I met Persica my first night in court. She was radiant in powder blue and her sparkling emerald eyes ensnared me at once."

Mira leaned closer, resting her elbows on the bed. "And? Who is the other?"

Prim rolled onto her back, eyes distant, dreamy. "Viola," she whispered, "is a vision. An everblooming flower. Persica is wilder—like an icy winter storm."

Mira let out a low whistle. "From Winter Court?"

Prim nodded, cheeks flushed. "Different houses. Different magic. But they make it work."

Mira leaned closer. "Is that even allowed?"

Prim grinned. "In Winter? Anything's allowed, if it's beautiful enough."

I smiled, letting her warmth wash over me, but something in her eyes—too bright—flickered like candlelight. It felt like watching a fairy-tale told a little too perfectly.

Mira exhaled a slow sigh, twisting a ring on her finger. "Maybe Faerie needs more of that."

I turned to study her. Mira had been spending a lot of time with Foxglove. They believed themselves discreet, but I had seen him sneaking down the unmarried female's hall on more than one occasion. I hadn't fooled myself into believing they were staying up talking.

All around me, it seemed fae were finding love. Something in my chest twinged at the thought. Banyan was nice enough, but I didn't think it would ever be love. A rush of air escaped me as I turned back to Prim. "If you weren't able to convince Mab, why did you come back?"

"The wedding. I must report my failed trip to my cousin and be in attendance for the ceremony of course." Prim's gaze dropped to the floor and I reached for her, squeezing her hand.

"You'll return to them soon, though I can't say I'm sad to have you back. At least for a little while."

Prim looked up, eyes brimming with wetness, but they cleared and she looked between us both. "Oh I've missed you! Not these dresses, though." She glanced down at her pastel yellow gown. "You would adore the fashion in Winter. It melts over your skin like soft petals."

"Speaking of dressing." I released her hand. "We should get dressed for the evening."

CHAPTER 27

Kaspar

*C*urrent day

Terror gripped me. A thread I hadn't realized I'd been holding all this time pulled taut—ready to snap.

I'd left her in Spring. With Sav. I thought she would be safe there.

My first instinct was to send spies into my uncle's court, but the ocean was a vast, dangerous place and I may be sending them to their death. Sage's wedding was tonight. Luck alone had released me from the autumn court's clutches in time to attend. As if our alliance wasn't strained enough, failing to show for the coronation of their new princess would cause irreparable damage.

I raced for land, sparing no time on an announcement or attire. Formality be damned.

Breaking the surface, I shifted quickly and galloped over mossy earth, through the Maywood and straight up to the palace door. Two orcs, strapped in a barrage of weapons, barred my path. "The wedding isn't until tonight, Prince. We have orders to restrict access until nightfall."

"Let me pass," I growled.

"Can't. General's orders."

I bared my teeth at them but neither flinched. They were well trained and would lay down their lives for their general. He inspired the kind of loyalty I dreamed of commanding one day. Perhaps in a century or two, my court would come to esteem me as the orcs did their general. Out of respect, I would not take them from him tonight.

"Give a message to one of the members of your court."

The orc on my right nodded, a silver eyebrow ring glinting in the morning sun.

"Tell Lady Briar to seek me out at once."

"The lady is being fitted for her dress, your highness."

"The other Lady Briar."

The orc nodded, asking no more questions.

Spinning on my heel, I ran around the side of the grounds. Sav was fast, but I wasn't sure when the message would be delivered or how quickly she could get out of the castle. I had another place to check before I prepared for war with my uncle.

Skirting the edge of the forest beside the west wing, the one I knew a certain prince resided in, I dropped low beside the spy master's window. When no sound came from his room, I hopped up, peering inside. Usually, I left spying to the hours when my extra gift was most useful, but I could waste no time when Mira may be in very real danger.

The room was empty. Not empty. It was a cluttered mess, but neither Mira nor Foxglove were inside.

My heart picked up speed. The hope that Mira had lied and was simply engaging in an amorous tryst with the prince was the only thing keeping me from cracking. If she had been truthful when she said she'd given him up, it left only one option. My uncle.

I turned, shifting, and raced away from the palace.

Beside the stream near Sav's cabin, the place we'd met for nearly two decades, I dipped a hand into the water, exhaling as the soothing magic calmed my taught muscles. If only I could open a portal and appear beside my uncle's castle as Mab could. But wishing for a thing and making it so were not the same. I peered into the tree line, searching for any sign of my princess and leaned back, gauging the sun's position in the sky.

I'd given her two hours and it was two hours more than I had to spare. I couldn't wait any longer. If I was wrong about this, I could be starting a war. One I wasn't prepared to win. But I couldn't leave my sister if he had her.

"Kaspar?"

I hopped up, searching for the owner of that voice.

"Sav."

She appeared between the trees, running for me and I raced to meet her. She crashed into me and I spun her, forgetting my worries just for a moment as our connection mended the fissure slowly tearing my heart in two these many weeks.

I set her down, letting her scent invade my senses, wrap around me, set the world right. Brilliant, purple eyes met mine and for a fraction of a second I was lost in them. Nothing and no one mattered. I shook the thought from my head. Someone did matter. Very much. "Mira. Where is she?" Sav's open expression shut down hard and irrational anger flared to life inside me. Sav knew. Sav knew where she was and she was prepared to lie to me. "Don't you dare."

She looked up at me, fear and regret swirling in her eyes. I wasn't sure who she was more afraid of losing though, me or Mira. "She only wants to be happy."

I ground my teeth, relishing the feel of the sharp points slicing into my gums. "She's with Foxglove."

"They have a plan."

"She is a subject of my court and as such must make her request to me." My hands balled into fists at my sides as I exhaled slowly. "Tell me where my sister is."

"Sister?"

My gaze shot up and red flashed in my vision as the male who thought to take what did not belong to him stepped out from behind a tree. If he was here it could only mean one thing.

"Mira!"

Indigo curls dipped out from behind another tree and her dark eyes met mine as she slunk forward reaching for the prince. I tracked the movement, eyes burning into the flesh wrapped around my sister's hand.

"Kaspar, they thought you might listen if I explained."

I stepped around Sav meeting Foxglove at the edge of the woods. "Mira. Come," I said, hoping, just for a breath, that she would obey as the members of my court were expected to.

Her face contorted, resolve twisting her features. "No."

Foxglove stood taller, grip tightening around Mira's. If I could have killed him where he stood without repercussions, he would be lifeless on the ground, but we had come close enough to war once and I would not lose my temper again. Now that I knew Mira was safe, it was only a matter of forcing her to see sense.

"Will you run away with him then? Spend your life as his mistress?"

Her chin raised and she met my eyes with cold defiance. "We will marry."

"He cannot marry you without the Queen's permission. You know she will never grant it. Not after Firethorn."

Mira's eyes glistened but she stood taller. "You don't know that."

"I do."

"We don't have to be married to make a life together."

My gaze darted back to Foxglove. "And you think your brother will allow you to remain unwed?"

A muscle in his jaw ticked but he said nothing.

Sav's scent slithered up my nostrils and her hand landed on my arm. Every fiber of my being strained to give her all my attention, but I would not give Mira the chance to use my emotions to her advantage. If she spoke the words I knew were bubbling on her tongue, I would be forced to kill her lover and I feared she would never forgive that.

"They are in love Kaspar. Let them go."

I ignored Sav's words, focusing on Mira once more. "He will be forced to marry. It is the duty of a prince. And when he does, you will be forced to choose. Give him up or share him. Are you prepared to do either?"

Mira's lower lip trembled.

"What if you were to become pregnant? Would you have the strength to end it?" My gut twisted, knowing how much those words would hurt, knowing she was all too aware of what such a dangerous thing would mean for her child. But I would rather spare her now than see her suffer later.

Her grip loosened and she dragged her eyes from mine, looking to Foxglove.

He searched her face. "Mira. Don't listen to him. We can take precautions. We'll never have to worry about that." She shook her head, taking a step back. "Mira?"

She blinked back tears, staring at him as if she were capturing every detail to file them away. I knew what it was to save the one you loved in the place no one could reach but you. To sit with them in the quiet hours and imagine what could be in another life. A piece of my heart cracked, breaking for my sister's unjust lot in life.

That he meant more to her than I'd imagined, only drove the knife in deeper. Would that I could tear these cursed hearts from our chests and leave duty to rule us instead. Then maybe we'd all survive what was coming.

CHAPTER 28

Sav

I bolted through the forest, vines snatching at my hair. There was no time to mourn Mira's pain, or to scold Kaspar for his cold, unfeeling words. My sister was getting married.

Rosemary shook her head and pointed to the bath when I appeared in the doorway to my room. Shoulders dipping, I slunk to the bathing room and slipped out of my torn, muddy gown. At least I'd had the good sense to change before I'd gone to meet him. If I'd ruined my gown for the wedding, Sage might have truly banished me from Spring.

I scrubbed quickly, rinsing away the evidence of my escape. At least now I knew how to do it. Foxglove had shown me the hidden passages in the library and kitchen and they would prove invaluable for however long I was forced to live at court. Until I was married. I'd be trapped in this palace with Alder's raging temper and the guards who never seemed far enough away for my liking.

A marriage to Lord Banyan was seeming better the more I weighed its merits.

Dinner with him had been underwhelming. A formal affair in one of the castle's dining rooms. I would have preferred a picnic under the stars, but it was clear he had made an effort. He'd even asked my sister what my favorite dish was and had it prepared especially for the evening.

Conversation was stilted as he felt it would be improper for us to sit beside one another and so we were forced to nearly shout down the table to attempt a dialogue. The rows of staff waiting along the wall also seemed unnecessary for just the two of us.

But it was the thought that counted. He had tried, and I told myself that mattered. Maybe once we got to know each other, we'd find more in common than silence and protocol. Maybe. His estate was large, filled with forests I'd never explored and bordered by Autumn. That court was a mystery I'd long dreamed of exploring. They were said to have some of the tallest waterfalls in Faerie and more than five types of trolls. Not to mention, the herbs there were something new to me and I would love to get a look at them.

It was against our laws to harvest from another court, but I could test a few without fear of anyone finding out, I was sure.

"Lady Briar. Time is short."

I sat up, jumping from the tub and splashing water in my wake.

In my room, Rosemary pinned my hair up, wrestling the wild mane into something befitting a lady of court and I marveled at my reflection in the mirror. She hadn't cuffed my ears or placed any jewels in my hair, instead sliding two simple pearl combs in to pull it off my face. It was perfect!

I stood, brushing out the soft fabric that split up my thigh to reveal just a bit of tanned skin. The gold belt cinched around my waist was a welcome reprieve from the corsets we were forced to wear day in and day out and the sheer gold material draping from my back almost appeared to be wings.

I spun in a circle. "Magical."

Rosemary's cheeks burned and I grinned. "Thank you, Rosemary."

She looked up. "I couldn't possibly, Lady."

"Of course you can. You've quite transformed me. Even my sister wouldn't be embarrassed tonight. Name your favor."

She gave me a shy smile, her tufted ear twitching beside her eye. "Well. There is one thing I wish for."

"When you marry Lord Banyan, take me with you." Her request struck something tender in me. I couldn't promise myself freedom—how could I promise it to her?

Sage moved as though born to the role of princess. Every gaze followed her, her gilded gown catching the afternoon sun as she glided down the long carpet, sheer golden fabric streaming behind her toward twin thrones.

I slipped into a seat at the back, brushing a tear from my cheek. Despite the chaos her betrothed had dragged with him, this was what Sage wanted. This male, this throne, this life. Pride swelled in my chest. For the first time in years, I wished our mother could have been here to see her. Father had come, and the red rim around his eyes told me he was thinking the same.

Her voice was steady as she repeated the words she'd rehearsed a dozen times with me, promising to put the needs of her folk and her court above her own. Her promise to remain by Alder's side till death and to never misuse his name.

I turned my expectant gaze on him, waiting for him to do the same, to promise to put the fae first and to guard my sister's true name against harm.

When the satyr rose ushering the couple to turn and face us, he still hadn't spoken. White hot rage twisted my gut. It was the one thing I'd expected from him. The one thing that would keep my sister safe.

And he hadn't made the bargain.

A dull sizzle started in my chest, trying to force its way down my arms, to light my palms on fire, but the oppressive poison coursing through my veins, coating my insides like oil-slicked vines, forced it into submission. Internally I raged. I would have burned him alive rather than see him wield such power over my sister, but her eyes met mine and narrowed.

I knew that look. *Stand down, Sav. This is my fight,* it said.

I looked away, catching sight of Kaspar, Mira beside him. Her eyes were puffy and blue. He whispered in her ear, and she glared at the side of his face. Not reconciled then.

Prim slid into the seat beside me and squeezed my arm. "I leave tomorrow," she whispered. "Come with me?"

My gaze swung to her. "I can't. My sister—"

"Your sister will be fine."

I shook my head. "She won't. He has her true name."

Prim looked down, swallowing.

"You knew." Rage clawed its way up my throat. I'd trusted her. Let her braid my hair and share my secrets, while she'd kept the most dangerous truth from me.

Her eyes met mine, shining. "I was sworn to secrecy. My cousin doesn't trust that Sage will do what's best for Spring." A tear trickled down her cheek. "I'm so sorry, Sav. I wanted to tell you."

The ache that followed was worse than anger. Worse than betrayal. It hollowed me. For years I'd told myself I had family and friends by my side. Now Sage had chosen her crown. Kaspar had wrapped himself in duty, Mira in her grief. And Prim—Prim had proven herself a Hawthorn after all.

There was no one left. No one I could lean on. No one I could trust.

I scooted back, out of Prim's reach. My voice was a whisper. "I should have known. I should never have trusted a Hawthorn."

She winced but pressed on. "He made a bargain. He would keep the night of Helenium's death a secret if I kept this from everyone. Especially you. And the other princes."

"The other princes?" The words tasted like ash. Why would they care? Why would anyone care but me? Then the truth slammed into me. "He was afraid they would object to the marriage."

Prim nodded, swiping her tears away.

"He never would have told anyone. It would have been worse for him if he had. That was a stupid bargain."

Her eyes narrowed, her voice sharp now. "Not all of us have princes who care for our welfare. Some of us have cousins who would sell us to another court to buy peace."

The words struck like a slap. My mouth opened, but nothing came. She rose and strode for the door, leaving me in silence.

I didn't call her back. What was left to say? I would not leave. Not until I was certain my sister was safe. And that no one, especially a Hawthorn, would wield her name against her.

CHAPTER 29

Kaspar

Mira trailed me, silent as we stepped into Spring's grandest ballroom. This room was reserved for special occasions, meant to hold the whole of the spring court. Crowded as it was, it should have been difficult to spy her, but no matter the size of space, I would always find Sav.

A male of average height and bland features had an arm wrapped possessively around her waist and my lip curled.

"A land and sea fae can never mix," Mira sneered in my ear.

I shrugged my shoulders, stepping away from my sister and her mood and stopped beside the couple. Sav looked over my shoulder, giving Mira a consoling look. "How are you?"

"The emissary is well," I said, drawing those amethyst eyes back to me. "She has chosen to spend more time in her home court to ensure she understands the values we represent before resuming her duties at court." Sav grimaced and my gaze shot to the hand trailing lazy circles on her arm. "Who is your companion?"

"Prince Kaspar, may I introduce Lord Banyan."

I filed the name away with a note to learn everything I could about the lord who was making his intentions more than clear. He dipped his head low and I smirked at the crown of his head. It was well that he knew his place with me. I would ensure he never forgot it.

"I need a drink," Mira announced, spinning on her heel and stomping away.

I gave Sav an apologetic look and turned to follow. I was not yet ready to let my sister wander freely in the spring court. She rolled her eyes at my approach.

"Must you stand so close?"

I lifted a glass to my lips. "If I see you with any princes, we will leave at once."

"I know."

I nodded, taking a small sip of my drink. Perhaps I was being too harsh on my sister. She'd made the choice to come home on her own and Foxglove was suspiciously absent tonight.

My gaze trailed the room, falling on auburn curls glinting in the fae-light. Rain began to fall, pattering against the glass ceiling, indicating it was midnight. The male beside her, Lord Banyan, tugged her reluctantly onto the dancefloor and I knew instantly from her stiff posture that she didn't want to go. He either didn't know her at all or didn't care and dragged her into a slow dance, one that was meant as more of a seduction than a light spin.

I watched them. The space she kept between them made her true feelings for him clear. A smile tugged at my lips. But if that was the case, why was she entertaining his attention?

Mira tapped her foot beside me, occasionally smashing my foot. If she'd matched the rhythm I might have been able to convince myself it wasn't intentional.

"Go. But stay with Sav and do not leave this ballroom. I *will* be watching."

If I had expected any form of gratitude I was mistaken. She trudged away, shoulders hunched. The pain in my chest that hadn't truly abated since I'd forced her to leave her prince in the forest intensified. She was young. She would recover. But perhaps love was not in my sister's future. She sought a partner who felt strong emotion as she did, not a sea creature whose heart was cold as ice, but such a thing would get her killed.

I may not be as old as many of my peers, but I knew one thing with absolute certainty. A heart was the one thing that could destroy you.

Mira cut in on Sav's dance and I had to press my glass to my lips to hide the smile. Lord Pompous turned three shades redder and I had to look away to keep from laughing out loud.

"Fancy finding you in a dark corner by yourself." I spun around, facing Primrose Magnolia. Her eyes left mine, trailing to the dance floor and she nodded, swiping a drink from the table. "I see."

My heart stuttered, but I remained perfectly still, cool gaze assessing her.

She glanced back and giggled. "You have nothing to fear from me. I am the queen of forbidden romances."

We stood in silence, sipping our drinks as we watched the crowd. My mind raced over all the recent events in my life. Autumn's seer, her revelations, now heavy in my mind, my uncle and the missing magic he was desperate to find. Sav and her new acquaintance. The fae beside me who always seemed to be lurking.

I was missing something, but I couldn't pin it down. The truth was a slippery thing, threatening to escape my grasp all together. I feared if I didn't discover the missing piece soon, I would pay for it.

Primrose's heart picked up speed and I followed her gaze to the door. Framed in fae light, and dusted in bronze powder, the raven-haired prince of summer stalked into the room. I tracked his progress knowing before he reached her who he was seeking.

I moved, but Primrose's arm shot up, gripping my biceps. "Don't."

The magic lacing her words had my own gifts rising to the surface and the dark swallowed us both in moments. She glanced around, eyebrows rising.

"Impressive."

I yanked my arm, but her fingers stuck. I looked down. "What magic is this?"

She grinned, a cold, brittle smile. "Something uniquely mine."

"Your family is cursed. You hold no great magic." I tugged again, but it was as if her fingers had suckers at their tips.

"I'll let you keep your secrets and you will allow me mine."

I tried to shake my head, but it was like moving through quicksand and I hissed, calling the water overhead to lend me strength.

"Be at ease, Prince Kaspar." Her words slithered in my ear. "He only wants to speak with her."

You're helping him? I tried to ask, but my lips wouldn't obey. Slowly, the dark receded and I stood motionless, Primrose's hand on my arm, holding me to the spot. If any were to glance our way, they would never assume the slight fae lightly touching me had the prince of Lakes and Streams locked in place.

When the darkness cleared and the room was fully visible again, I scanned the dancefloor searching for Sav, Fero and... Mira. My gaze darted from the dancers to the alcoves beside them. Most were closed, obscuring my view but those that weren't held only courtiers I didn't recognize. I swiveled my gaze left then right trying to shout, to scream for her to release me.

Where had he taken them? What had he done with Sav and my sister?

The magic is my veins strained against her odd gift, prodding for weak spots but it was as if she'd wrapped me in ten layers of skink worm thread. My eyes were the only thing free. I looked up begging whatever deity my kind owed fealty to to break a pane of glass and call the magic giving water to my aid, but no matter how I raged inside, on the outside, I was the cool, indifferent prince.

Primrose turned, as if remembering I existed. Her hand dropped. She stumbled back, bumping a table and knocking over a glass.

Whatever spell had held her shattered.

And so did I.

All the fury building inside me burst free—air magic tearing outward in every direction. Fae were blasted off their feet, plates and tables flung against the walls.

Overhead, the glass ceiling exploded. The sky obeyed. Rain surged through the wreckage, striking my skin like a promise of vengeance as shards spiraled to the floor and folk screamed, scrambling for cover.

Water whipped through the room in a cyclone, scattering glass like wind-blown blades.

The storm pummeled my skin, raising every hair on my arms as raw power coursed through me.

Wind roared, beating the rain into a frothing tumult. I inhaled, rolling my neck as energy snapped through my limbs. My gaze swept the ballroom, hunting.

Fero.

CHAPTER 30

Sav

My vision swam in and out of focus. Above me loomed a face I was coming to know too well. I glanced around, squinting in the onslaught of rain. My first thought was that it never rained this hard in Spring. My second was that I was being carried.

I tried to fight his grip, but he pinned me against his chest, jogging through the gardens toward the maze. "Prince... Fero..." My words were sluggish and weak. "Put... me... down."

He glanced down, but kept running. Hedges caught in my hair ripping strands free. I tried to lift my arms, to press flaming palms against his bare skin, but my arms were like tree trunks, immovable. I giggled and tried in vain to close my lips. Why was I giggling? What was so funny?

We stopped and the world spun dangerously. The hedge walls pulsed, too green and too close. Flowers blinked in and out of focus like white and pink stars. Bile burned up my throat and I choked out a sob. He looked down again and swore, tipping me on my side. Dark liquid splattered the white petals lining the hedges boxing us in and I grimaced as my head cleared a little.

"Fight it," the prince commanded.

168

He took me. That thought sliced through the haze sharp and terrifying. *Mira.* Was she here too? Another burst of dark salty liquid burbled over my lips.

He moved, carrying me to the center of the maze, and laid me down on the grass. The grass felt cold. Or maybe it was my skin that had gone hot. I couldn't tell anymore. The world was spinning by, the prince's face circling me menacingly. I opened my mouth, tasting blood. He lifted my arms, running my fingers over sharp spikes.

No. Please, I tried to beg, but my eyes had closed and I struggled to hang on to consciousness.

Wetness splattered my face and I coughed. It was a dry hack, only the taste of old blood coating my throat. Flashes of light streaked across the sky illuminating the view before me. A vortex of wind and water swirled around Kaspar, bending shrubs and trees under the force of his power.

The world narrowed to a pinprick of sound. Kaspar's name echoed, muffled and distant, like it was trapped underwater.

Darkness.

Prince Fero raised his arms overhead. The sky split open. Blinding flashes lit the chaos as lighting found its mark—Kaspar. When the light faded, Kaspar crumpled, steam rising from his shoulders like smoke off scorched stone.

Darkness.

"Kaspar," I tried to say. It came out as a breath. *Please don't kill him.* My limbs twitched. My eyes burned. I was drowning in black.

Don't die, I thought. *Don't you dare die.*

I cracked heavy lids. Something soft swatted the hair on my face. I blinked, peeling my lids apart and trying to keep them open. Large yellow eyes blinked down at me. I tilted my head. "Jessica?"

Ivy's cat yowled ferociously and jumped off her perch running out of the room.

"Sav!" Ivy came into the room towering over me. "Prince. Come quick. She's awake!"

My muddy brain fumbled for answers. Why was I back in Ivy's home? What had I done this time? I wiped my eyes, clearing the crust away. Had I been crying?

Aquamarine eyes appeared in the door and Kaspar dropped beside me, wrapping cool hands around my much warmer ones. I tried to smile, but tiny burning sores lined my mouth as though I'd tried to eat a cactus. I opened my mouth, but he spoke first.

"Where's Mira?"

CHAPTER 31

Kaspar

Sav grimaced as she tried to speak around the sores left behind after her near death incident with poison. It was a very particular poison, derived from squid ink and it was my only clue to Mira's whereabouts.

I would have marched on my uncle immediately, but it wasn't a sea fae spy absconding with Sav the night of the ball. It was Prince Fero. All my early suspicions had immediately resurfaced. I'd thought it was possible they were working together, but what if it was so much worse than that? What if Fero was the mastermind behind it all?

I knew about his gift, the ability to steal from others and use it for himself. A gift like that had unimaginable possibilities. Primrose had said he only wanted to talk. But she had bought him time to poison Sav and take Mira. Was Mira my uncle's price for alliance? Or was she, even now, trapped in Summer?

"Please Sav, I know you've suffered, but I must know who took Mira."

Her brow furrowed and she held a hand to her head, trying to sit up. I pressed my palm against her back to guide her, and she leaned heavily against my arm, back still dangerously warm. If only I hadn't brought her that tea. Her magic would have burned away the poison. Instead, she fought its effects even now. Squid ink poison could be lethal to water folk, but it was almost certainly a death sentence for land fae. Even my blood, washed down her throat in two-hour intervals, hadn't completely restored her.

If she couldn't fight the magic raging inside her, she could be permanently injured. There was no telling how severe the damage might be, or what it would cost her.

She coughed, small flecks of blue and red blood landing on my cheek.

I rubbed circles on her back, torn between wanting to nurse her through it and the desperate need to find my sister. "Please. Anything you can remember."

She nodded, bending forward, head lolling between her knees. "Fero," she gasped.

"Yes. I know he was involved. But he was with you. Who took Mira?"

She sat up, hand landing on my shoulder and leaning on me. Our eyes met and hers were so dim ice sliced through me. Would she lose her magic? I'd never heard of such a thing, but eyes that dull...

"He... handed her... a... drink..."

"Ivy!" The healer appeared beside me and I lifted Sav's hand gingerly, pressing it into Ivy's outstretched palm. "Take care of her."

She nodded and I stood, pressing a light kiss to Sav's forehead.

"I'll return." I spared one last look at my princess before turning and racing for my court.

At the center of my lake floor, I called the captain and the entire guard. When they floated in uniform lines, I searched the legion for the shifters among them, beckoning them forward.

"Summer is a fool to think he can outlast me. His court will crumble without access to water."

The legion stared ahead, awaiting my command.

"But time is not on our side. Even now, they may be torturing her."

They floated.

"I will do the thing they least expected. I will drown them where they stand."

My shifters formed a line in front.

"Shifters. When I pull back the streams running through their land, attack."

"Yes, Highness!"

"Water guard. When I bring the waves, go for their throats. Don't give them a chance to reach the surface."

"Yes, Highness!"

I nodded once. My plan was full of holes, not the least of which was a prince who wielded water all on his own. I was betting on surprise. He had proven last night that his magic was greater on land. We would see who commanded water.

Shifting, my hoof scraped the sea glass floor and my legion stiffened. I snorted once. Twitching both ears, I called the current inside my veins. Muscles bulging, I pulled with all my strength on the threads snaking through summer. Heaving, I stepped back and water retreated. I took another step back and another. Waves crashed overhead as the lake swelled, and my shores were buried beneath the weight of all that water.

I snorted again and my shifted warriors leaped into action, racing upstream.

When they had disappeared, I nodded to Alaco. Millions of silver fish circled me, vicious teeth gnashing. Leaning down, I sliced my chest, letting the dark blood fill the water. It worked as desired, inciting the mob and they raced for the surface.

I spared a moment to steady my nerves.

The swirling sparkling army circled higher, and I released my hold on the current facing Summer's shores. It broke like a dam, racing for Summer's castle. If they were holding her, this would be her moment to break free.

When they swarmed with the tide, I raced after them, charging across the lakebed, pulling more water with me. Overtaking them in moments, I charged ahead, dragging waves behind me. The summer court came into view and I galloped faster, angry water frothing at my hooves as I charged for my enemy.

We reached the open palace, free of glass or impediment and the force of my wave slammed sandstone, traveling through pillars, submerging every crevice. I raced through and out the other side, stumbling to a halt. There were no screams, no cries for help, no blood in the water.

They had expected us.

We reached the sparkling beach on the other side and a garbled shout escaped my lips. I shifted, letting the water carry me to her as I fell into the briny water, scooping her limp body into my arms. Her skin was waxy, her mouth slightly open as though she'd tried to scream.

"Mira!"

The crack through my center was audible as I hugged her limp form against me and screamed again. "Mira. Mira." I pulled her onto the shore and laid her gently on the sandy beach. Her dark eyes were wide, a look of shock frozen into her features. My gaze drifted south, mind struggling to process the sight of her torn flesh and the gaping hole where a heart once lived.

My forehead dropped to hers and I pressed her lids down over sightless eyes, a keening wail escaping my lips.

"Sire." The tentative voice of one of my shifter warriors drew me up short and I gasped a broken breath, desperate to compose myself. "Sire. The legion. They can't survive."

I tore my gaze from my sister's sallow form, bleary eyes taking in the flopping mass of bodies baking in the summer heat. They sucked desperately for water, some already stilling. Without me to hold the water, it had drained away quickly, leaving my creatures to suffocate on land.

A trap. It had been a trap and I had fallen directly into it. Lifting Mira in my arms, I marched through my dying army, seeking the nearest freshwater current. The ocean at my back called to me, screamed for me to command it, but it would kill my army as quickly as the sun.

I stepped over Alaco's still form, numbness washing over me.

I was a fool, a young, inexperienced fool playing a game I couldn't win. I had drained the only freshwater within reach. My foe had anticipated my reaction. Had known what would happen when I found Mira on the beach. I moved as if traveling upstream, weighed down by my failure and the court I had destroyed in one fell swoop.

I walked on fae legs, the blistering heat baking the soles of my feet and searched in vain for any sign of life giving water.

When the sand changed to a light green grass, interspersed with pebbles and stones I tried again. There. It was distant, but I felt it. Called to it and it answered, rushing over land, carving a new path toward me. I set Mira down and shifted, careful not to crush her under foot and reached deep within, dragging every drop of water from the stream bisecting Spring and Autumn.

I was too late. I knew. But I would not give up on them. Just as I had not given up on Mira until the bitter end.

Leaning down, I nudged Mira's limp body onto my nose, tossing her up and onto my back, then I carried her on a wave of water back to Summer. Desperate to save even one of the soldiers that I had sent to their death.

THE END

EPILOGUE

Sav

Three months later

I cleared my throat, raising my hands for the court to see. Fero's marigold eyes gleamed in the crowd and I swallowed the lump rising in my throat. I spread both fingers wide, looking to the proctor for confirmation. He nodded and I let the trickle of magic in my veins flare to life. Twin balls of flame burst into my palms shooting sparks into the sky before settling comfortably.

"Fire," the proctor announced. "Now, show us full power."

I straightened my shoulders. I had puzzled over today a dozen times. On the one hand, great power would mean respect from those at court. On the other, it could mean those like Fero would search for ways to use me. If I'd learned anything in my short time at court, it was that I was unprepared to play the games of nobles and royals.

Better to blend in. Better to let them believe my only value was in my relationship to my sister. Then only the least powerful at court would vie for my favor.

I pushed against the magic still bound by the tea Kaspar had given me. The thought of him sent a fresh pang through my chest. He had promised he would return.

After I'd nearly died—my recovery slow and agonizing—I'd learned of Mira's death. Not from him. From Sage. The loss itself had gutted me, but learning it secondhand, not from my oldest friend, carved a wound deeper still. One I wasn't sure would ever close.

I couldn't fault him for grieving, but I couldn't understand his silence. Word reached us at court of his army's ruin, wiped out in a single blow. Perhaps that was why he stayed away; trapped in his lake, guarding broken borders against an enemy none of us had yet seen.

My gaze cut back to Prince Fero, narrowing. Most of that night blurred in my mind, but one memory burned clear. His hand offering Mira and me our cups. Poison disguised as wine. Enough to snuff out the brightest light in Faerie.

I shut my eyes against the surge of grief. I only had to endure today. Then I could retreat to my room. To silence. To solitude.

When I opened them again, my flames licked higher. Impressive enough for a fire fae, yet hollow. Something inside me had shifted. The fire was still there, but it no longer answered the way it once had.

"Is that all?" The proctor eyed my mediocre display.

Prince Fero was no fool. He'd sensed my magic. I had to do better if I were to convince him that what he'd felt was real, if not as great as he'd assumed.

I pushed harder, sparks streaming into the sky. It took more effort than I'd like to admit and I didn't know if it was the tea that had never seemed to clear from my system, or the poison that nearly killed me, but whatever great magic I'd been suspected of having, it was gone now.

A few folk in the front row gasped. *Good.*

I glanced at the prince of Summer once more. His brows were dark slashes on his forehead. He stood and several fae looked his way. In true Fero fashion, he paid them all no mind, stepping over folk as he marched for the exit.

I hoped it was the last I'd see of him. I hoped it had been enough to convince him I wasn't a threat to him.

"Fero."

All eyes spun to the back as Kaspar appeared and raised both arms.

Water crashed behind him, rising like a wall of judgment.

"Face me."

My gaze darted to my old friend, heart shattering. In three months, he was changed. Darker. Gaunt in a way he'd never been before. The look in his aquamarine gaze was harder than it had ever been. If any emotion lived in my friend, it had been ripped away when Mira was taken from him.

The prince turned to him calmly, but made no move to call on his own magic.

"I am not your enemy, Prince."

"As long as you draw breath, I will see you as nothing else."

My throat dried. Prince Fero's hands rested at his sides. There was a cold restraint in his stance that spoke of his level headed calculation. He was not in his court or his enemy's. He was in mine. War on our soil was war with Spring. I was certain it was the only reason he had not attacked.

My gaze flicked to Sage as she stood from her place in the front row and turned toward our oldest friend. We had delayed my ceremony, in favor of allowing Sage to show her magic to the court first. In truth, we'd been buying time for my magic to return.

"You are welcome in my court, Prince Kaspar. But use your magic on my guests and you will find yourself at odds with both your borders."

My sister raised a hand and a jagged fissure opened up between Kaspar and the guests who had come to my ceremony. Several gasped, backing up as rocks and debris fell into the chasm she had just created. Kaspar could send his waves over it of course, but it would not flood the grounds.

"Order Prince Fero off your land or find yourself at war with your closest neighbor. I will not hesitate to cut off your water supply."

Sage straightened her shoulders even as several fae choked back murmurs of disbelief. This was the kind of callous behavior that had set land

and sea at odds all those centuries ago. Before Mab divided the realm into seasons that forced our cooperation.

"Do it and you will live in a state of perpetual quakes of which your castle will not survive." Her voice didn't quiver, but I knew her well enough to hear the unease in it. "With your soldiers so depleted can you hope to defend against us both?"

Prince Fero raised his hands and Sage and Kaspar both swiveled their gazes to the greatest threat. "I will go."

Sage closed her mouth and I was grateful. Three powerful fae fighting with the might of their gifts would destroy much of the land and the weaker creatures gathered here today. I had known my sister would step into her role, but I had not been prepared for her power. It was great, indeed.

The three stared at one another, each with their hands raised.

Prince Fero's gaze shot to me. "I didn't do it."

Before I could utter a word he clapped his hands together and was gone.

I stared dumbfounded at the space where he'd been. A dark slash through the air, roughly the size of the prince, gaped wide, sandy dunes visible in the distance. I leaned closer to inspect it. As quickly as it had appeared, it was gone, leaving only a scorched patch of earth in its wake.

I looked up, but Kaspar had departed, taking his wall of water with him.

Leaving the stand, I dropped to the uneven earth beside Sage. She stood at the edge of the chasm, staring at flattened tulips cutting a path to the forest beyond our court. She glanced at me.

"We cannot have them both as enemies." My gaze trailed down her arms, catching sight of the dark pooling at the tips of her fingers and she quickly wrapped her hands under her arms to stop their trembling. "I cannot defend against them both."

I wrapped an arm around her. And I... I didn't know if I could stand between them either.

Read more in Poison Amidst Bloom

READ A PREVIEW OF
POISON AMIDST BLOOMS

Read the first three chapters of Poison Amidst Blooms for free!

BOOKS BY CASSANDRA ASTON

Prophecies of Angels and Demons

> ***Grave Secrets*** *– book 1*
> ***Firefly*** *– Simon's Novella – book 1.5*
> ***Grave Prophecies*** *– book 2*
> ***Light*** *– Gabriel's Novella – book 2.5*
> ***Grave Revelations*** *– book 3*
> ***Parable*** *– Peter's Novella – book 3.5*
> ***Fated*** *– Sanura's Kindle Vella*

Deadly Fae Duology

> ***Whispers Among Thorns***
> ***Spring*** *– Book 1.5*

Poison Amidst Blooms
Winter – *Book 2.5*

The Drowned Fae Realms (Deadly Fae Continuation)

Book 1 – *Coming 2027*

Vicious Villains: A Twisted Fairytale Reimagining Anthology Series

Book 1 – *Coming 2026*

THANK YOU

Thank you for reading Spring. If you enjoyed this book, please consider leaving an honest review on your favorite store.
To leave a review on Amazon

To leave a review on Goodreads

CASSANDRA ASTON

Check out everything I'm working on or sign-up up for my newsletter on my website

Acknowledgments

If you've made it this far, a special thank-you to you. Readers like you are the reason I keep going!

To Brittni and my mom, for being the first people to read my horrible drafts and for reading it again and again as I worked through all the small details.

To Frankie, for sticking with me through another series. I appreciate all you do.

To my content team, for all your support throughout the series and for endlessly shouting about my stories to anyone who will listen.

To my son, who tells everyone he meets about my books, sometimes to my embarrassment. Thank you for being my biggest supporter. The cat is named for you. ;)

To Tivuel for creating such beautiful art and for inspiring me to write Kaspar's story. And to the other artists for creating gorgeous art of Sav, Jack, and the rest of the characters in the Deadly Fae series.

To Laura for creating the beautiful hardcover editions of the series.

To Nicole and Kelly, my editing ninjas. I appreciate all you do to help bring my stories to life. I think we're all Team Kaspar, for better or worse.

Thank you.

ABOUT THE AUTHOR

I write dark fantasy and romantic fantasy for readers who want both. Plot that keeps you turning pages at 2 am and romance that ruins you for everyone else.

My books always feature a fierce heroine, emotionally complex characters, and the kind of dark, difficult themes that stay with you long after the last page. But don't worry, no matter how twisted the journey gets, I'll always bring you home to a happy ending at the end of the series. I can't promise the same for novellas.

If you love Ilona Andrews or K.F. Breene, you'll feel right at home.

I write from Houston, Texas, escaping to the mountains whenever I can, fueled by hot chocolate and spite.